SHE-WOLF AND CUB

She-Wolf and Cub

Lilith Saintcrow

INTEGRATED MEDIA
NEW YORK

ISBN: 979-8-3372-0838-1

This edition published in 2026 by Open Road Integrated Media, Inc.
180 Maiden Lane
New York, NY 10038
www.openroadmedia.com

SHE-WOLF AND CUB

PROLOGUE

MATERNAL TYPE

The bar was dim, full of fauxsmoke. Modern ersatz cigs don't kill you like the old ones, and synthetic liquor doesn't bite either. Everything's cushioned, to keep warmbodies from hurting themselves.

In return, they keep their heads down and their shoulders to the wheel. So do we.

Across from me, wheat-haired Sam slumped, staring at the amber fluid in his glass as if the ice cubes were going to suddenly spell out a message from on high.

Maybe they were. His washed-out gray eyes shone briefly, a reflection of blue neon. The iris pigments have to be original, for some reason nanos won't touch them. Still, within certain canons, you can get what you want once you're implemented. You can be striking, but not distinctive.

"Do this," he said finally, *"and you'll be quits."*

I blinked at the picture. Nice-looking kid, maybe eight or nine, an engaging gap-toothed smile and a big, vertical, surgical scar on his chin. Thick dark hair cut straight across his forehead. He was frowning slightly, not looking into the camera, everything around him blurred. Telephoto, probably, and black and white.

Color exposes things. Like the shadow on the kid's cheek. Bruise or dirt or something else. Didn't matter. Not to me, or so I told myself.

Paper's still best for this kind of work. The glorious future's swimming in it, even if it's made from reshuffled organic waste instead of precious tree fibers. It burns, and then it's deleted. Not like anything electronic. Convenience means trackability.

I slid the glossy 8x10 back into the envelope. *"What is this shit?"*

Fauxsmoke fug made a good frame for Sam's head. *"Control knows your feelings. They're prepared to do certain things to overcome them."*

No reason to take kid jobs, that's my personal view. Stay in the shadows and stay out of the under-18 pool, that's just good business sense, in love, war, work, what-have-you. Having rules is dangerous—you start following the rule instead of thinking—but at the same time, you need some guides when you're a liquidator or you go right off the rails.

A fully-implemented agent going off the rails is just begging for Dismissal. So you just put your nice, technologically redone, almost-invulnerable skull down and do what they want. It's the safest course.

"There is no overcoming my feelings." I slid the envelope across the table; it bumped the bottom of his sweating drink. His lips thinned. *"There are agents who don't mind that work. I do."*

"Triple your fee, and quits. Or you can move into Facilitation."

"I don't want a desk job." I didn't add the codicil. *And I don't owe you or the Agency anything.*

Not that "owe" really entered into it. "Own," on the other hand, did. Such a tiny change, one little letter, and you had unvarnished truth. I'd figured that out on my own, smart girl that I am.

"Clean slate. Untraceable identity."

"Please." How untraceable, if you're giving it to me? You think I'm stupid? "I said no, Sam."

I don't know if *Sam* is his name. I picked it because I had to call him something, just like he picked a name for me, and he'd been my handler ever since the Agency decided I was indeed useful enough to warrant the cost of implementation.

I wondered how many other agents he had. Sometimes.

He looks so average, Sam's the only name that applies. Not Joe, because Joe Smith, really? Not John, because that's so Freudian. But Sam Smith? The alliteration makes a good peg to hang him on.

"Jess." He even said it kindly, staring at his glass. *"You can't say no."*

Referring to me that way instead of with a number, or as *Agent*. Interesting.

Heartbeat, respiration, glandular balance all stayed the same. My glucose uptake spiked a little, the brain inside its lovely indestructible casing perking up. Galvanic skin response stayed flatline, though. Full implementation gives you near-perfect control over the body's autonomic. You have to start watching for psychological "tells" instead of physiological ones.

Dear old Sammy, fully implemented too, was flatline as well. After you're redone, well, you're just the messenger. Doesn't pay to shoot you, though they pretty much always try. Doesn't pay to kick, because the Agency always kicks harder. Doesn't pay to do anything but toe the line, ride the rail, nod and yessir, grin and bear it.

"I don't do kids." It surprised even me. For one thing, I'd used audible communication instead of the subvocal grumble that's standard for meets. For another, I put a finger on the envelope and shoved it, again, the sturdy wet paper crinkling a little as it pushed his glass. Another fractional application of force, and the drink would end up in his lap.

Unless implemented reflexes kicked in.

"Keep it down." He stayed subvocal, and that irritated me.

Audible again, this time consciously. "Is this how you got into Facilitation?"

"None of your business."

Score one for me, I'd forced him to shift to audible too. Bonus, he even looked irritated. I decided against dumping his drink in his lap. "There are other agents." There are *always* other agents.

A shrug. He spread his hands on the tabletop, nice manicured fingernails, cared for but not overly femme. Everything in moderation. It was probably why he was in Facilitation instead of actual work.

"Control decided on you." *I'm just passing the news along, his tone said, plainly. Don't get irrational.* "Refusal will mean Dismissal."

"You're not serious." Sometimes, you just have to take refuge in cliché.

"Sadly, yes." As if he was anything else, ever.

I settled back in my chair. Looked out over the restaurant again, with its checkered tablecloths and its smells of ersatz and human sweat.

It would do no good to rip his head off right now. He would just get reattached, unless I dropped it in a vat of something corrosive enough. Even if I did, it would only buy me a little time. They could broadcast a killcode; I wasn't stupid enough to think we'd found *every* implanted dismiss switch in my reinforced bones and enhanced muscles.

Even if I had, there would be operatives after me, the whole City would be a trap, and it wouldn't be personal.

Nothing ever is.

"Why?" It surprised me, hearing the unanswerable come out of my own mouth. I hadn't asked such a stupid question since my intake interview, back when I was a frightened little warmbody. "I mean, why this kid? What about his parents?"

Sam sighed. He reached up and pinched the bridge of his completely nondescript nose. It was by far the most emotion he'd ever shown.

Then he told me.

I started laughing. Audibly. Loud enough that a couple smoke-puffing warmbodies eating late lunch or early dinner glanced in our direction, incuriously. The vapor probably deadened the taste of sythprotein.

I'd like to say it was then I decided, but I'd be lying. When I took the job, I had every intention of seeing it through.

The first step is always to watch. Some fully-implemented assholes think *practically indestructible* means *run in like an idiot and waste resources*—not just ammunition but time, effort, emotion.

Just because you can control the autonomics doesn't mean you don't feel anything. I wish they would've told me that when I "volunteered" for the process. Then again, I wouldn't have cared—I had to get out of the Projekts, and quick. I look and sound nothing like I did, but every time I venture into the crumbling concrete tenements I have to clamp a subroutine over my heartrate, so I don't end up feeling young, warmbodied, and terrified all over again.

This wasn't the Projekts, though. This was a nice suburban Ring street, live trees and all. Static gens on each corner to keep the air a little cleaner, so the greenery didn't bend and die under a choking layer of ground-smog. The houses had permabrick faces; it took serious money to look like the antique middle class nowadays. This entire neighborhood was joint-corporate-owned, what they used to call company housing. The houses don't all look the same, but the differences were all of the same kind.

The kid's house was middle of the block. I settled across the street, in a hypergrown tree—it looked like a birch crossed with something, but I didn't bother to test its helix to find out. My camosuit matched its shifting shades, but I might as well have been naked. Precious few warmbodies think to look *up*. The permanently cloudy bowl of the City's sky isn't very attractive. Some said that out in the Waste there's desert sunshine, but I didn't know.

Not then.

A sleek silver railbus paused at the corner. A gaggle of schoolkids, all in corporate uniform, tumbled out. Navy blazers, the crest of their parents' corp owners stitched in shimmer-thread, trousers for boys and plaid skorts for girls. The A-gens were already the loudest, each one with a coterie of Bs taking their cues from the dominants. The rest fell elsewhere on the scale, gamma, epsilon, but there was one they all avoided—a thin, gangly kid with a cap of dark hair and a NifulCorp badge on his blazer.

The camosuit ruffled, having to work a little harder because I'd gone too still. My instinctive shifting, mimicking the tree's motion as an unsteady breeze flirted with its force-grown green branches, had paused.

Was it then? Every once in a while I replay the moment, searching for an internal seismic event. I don't know, even now. I watched, now making fractional movements with the tree, as one of the A-gens shouted at the dark-haired boy.

"Scar-face!" The A-gen, a freckle-faced redhead who had probably just squeaked past the border into management

material, added a few more. *"Retard! Freak!"* The taunts flew with a snatched-up stone.

The dark-haired kid's head snapped aside. I lifted the nocs, carefully, swept the entire group of kids. Some of the Bs blanched, the other kids shied away, and one of the other As—a girl with long light platinum hair that had to have been coded in—made a face. I read her lips. *Leave him alone, Croy.*

Croy didn't think so. *"Got a girlfriend, freak?"*

A thread of bright crimson traced down the kid's cheek. His eyes were big and bright, and the hate in them was clearly visible. Or maybe I was just projecting, because I would have fought back, even at that tender age.

This kid didn't. He just hitched his backpack up and trudged down the street, away from the now-laughing group of B-gens around Croy the redhead.

I dropped the nocs. They dangled against my chest. *Huh.* NifulCorp was heavy-duty genetics, they worked hand in glove with the Agency on some aspects of implementation. They also did a lot of embryonic coding, building better babies for those who could afford them. Nothing like a good solid legal coding to set your child off on the right foot—or an expensive and technically illegal one if you wanted said kid to have a leg up.

A couple more pebbles hit the sidewalk behind the dark-haired boy, with desultory clipping sounds. He put his head down, thin shoulders slumping. The posture should have shouted *victim*. Unfortunately, there was a certain arrogance to it, probably fuel to the fire when facing unsteady A-gens.

Scuffed brogans, frayed hems on his trouser-legs, his collar was shabby and his blazer worn at the elbows. Puzzling. The kid was a significant investment, and they let him run around like this?

Investment or not, I had a job to do. It wouldn't take much

time at all. Could have done it already, if I'd wanted to make a scene. But no, quick and relatively quiet was the order.

He climbed the steps, head still down, and put his thumb on the printlock. I heard the click all the way across the street, my senses dialed up and pinpointed. Croy was still loafing at the end of the block with his coterie, laughing loudly. The others had begun to peel away in smaller groups, only the closest in status or relationship to the A-gens walking with them. The platinum girl flipped her hair pertly over her shoulder, a nice balanced group of Bs buzzing around her. She'd probably breezed right through the initial dominance tests.

"Geoffrey." His name, breathed out subvocally. I almost twitched, not realizing it had come from me.

The kid couldn't have heard, but he halted as the doorlocks chucked open in response to the printlock's nudging, and looked over his shoulder.

Those eyes. Huge, and dark, and . . .

What? Haunted? That was absurd. There was no such thing.

Of course, there was no such thing as *him*, either. Yet there he was, in broad, even if UV-free, daylight, that scar on his chin quivering a little. Why hadn't they reconstructed it better? They had the tech, and if he was what Sam had said, a creature right out of sims and fairytales, this made no sense.

I was thinking too much. I should have just done it then.

Instead, I went to see Barlowe.

Pop-fizzing of static-laden gunfire, lots of cheap blue neon, the smog close and choking building a layer of grime on all surfaces. Everyone who can afford them wears nasal filters. It makes the Projekts a land of silver-proboscis insects, hurrying back and forth, ducking when flying ammunition passes overhead like a wave. Rooftops belong to druglords and runners, whole wars fought over certain streets or desirable vantage points.

Agents don't need filters. Still, every time I ventured into the Projekts, I wore them, partly to fit in and partly because, well, why make it harder on the nanos? They recharge themselves, renew the body, they're every little practically-immortal's helper, and after a while I felt pretty protective of mine. I'm just a skin sack for the whole beneficial colony to carry itself around, but still.

The Agency can't broadcast a killcode to your own nanos, the survival imperative's too strong. So it was the implanted dismiss switches, and scans could find most of those suckers, even the most ingeniously-hidden. Of course, more could be inserted, if you got maintenance or reworking. A lot of agents figure, oh well, the Agency keeps you in the red as a matter of course, might as well get upgraded and add to your debt.

Stupid.

Barlowe had deactivated a clutch of hidden switches I didn't know existed inside my flesh, and I paid him untraceable hard bitcoin and information for the service. Still, he survived in the Projekts. It would be idiotic to not leave a few in me, just for insurance.

I hunched my shoulders and hurried along, mimicking the crowd's flow. Dirt-colored caftan, grime smeared on my face, the corroded silver glints of new nasal filters reworked to seem old, I was just another anonymous hustling bit of scurryware. I surfaced at the Rawlin Ave. station and kept working my way, meandering, to Cirquit Quartah. There wasn't any point in going directly to him. Make every move as if you're being tracked, that's just good tactics.

It makes the times you slip the leash and drop off the grid much better. Sometimes I even do it randomly, sometimes I do it and pop up in the same place. If the Agency *is* watching I want to be normal. No agent ever goes without breaking the leash a few times, or trying to.

Every agent has shadowside contacts. If you stuck to only the official ones you'd be Dismissed for ineffectiveness soon enough. Barlowe, though, wasn't quite officially unofficial enough.

For one thing, I wasn't sure who owned him. A couple corporations *thought* they did, but the more I dug—oh, very carefully, respectfully, to be sure—the less I knew. If he wasn't owned, or if he was only *slightly* owned, well. That was interesting.

Nobody's free anymore. I wasn't even sure anyone had ever been. Even cannibals out in the Waste had to trade with City scrappers, or so I heard.

Anyway, I slid into Cirquit and dropped off the tracking grid in a new way, ducking through a Phan Tong restaurant and the smoky steam-hell of the kitchen, cheap stathydroponic produce and vat-grown proteins slathered with synthetic seasonings imitating what it used to taste like. Or just someone's idea of what it used to taste like. It could break your brain to think about too deeply.

Barlowe was now in a repurposed railbus hanging over Martell, deep in the Cirquit. He looked up and grunted as I slid through the bead curtain hanging just inside the regular entryway, a skinny old white-haired man with ancient hyperalloy implants at knees and elbows. A scan would show him as only a little implemented, not even up to a minimum security standard for a drugrunner or a corporate officer. He had an ocular over one eye, good work without a tag. That was another thing—his implementation wasn't even back-alley registered. It was completely innocent of anything approaching a serial.

Which meant the Agency would hotlist him in a split second.

They're the power they are because of their stranglehold on implementation; even illegals pay them. One way . . . or another.

"There she is," Barlowe rasped. His nose was incredibly long, and he scrubbed the back of his liver-spotted right hand under it. "My little wind-up girl. What'll it be? What have you brought old Papa?"

"Good afternoon, sir." I'd found him through a contact I had to liquidate a few years ago. Poor old Pinok, just smart enough to get into a game he was too dumb to survive in. "How are you feeling?" Soft and polite was the best way to handle the cranky old bastard.

"Oh, she wants something *big*, does she? What now? Only visits when she needs things. Ungrateful little girl." He jabbed a finger at me, stained orange-ish by ersatz nicotine. His fluff of white hair was a rooster's tail, lifted high and proud. Not that I'd ever seen a rooster except on packets of Copona cigarettes, but still.

"I can leave." I turned aside to study the glass case near the door. Little trinkets scattered across stained silvery tinselcloth; he had a legitimate pawner's license and paid his bribes to enforcement punctually. "If you're busy, sir."

He snorted a very rude term, shuffled around his counter. One claw shot out, closed around a half-full bottle of ersatz rye. He took a healthy draft of it, scrawny throat working, before offering me the bottle.

I lifted it to my lips, politely, but as usual he didn't check to see if I drank. Instead, he went past me and bolted the door, turned the ancient sign with its old-fashioned blonde pinup girl showing her warmbody ass to *Closed*, and shuffled back for the counter. "Come back. Might as well scan you while you're here. Though you're clean."

"Maybe." I carried the bottle back. "Sir, I have a question."

"Oh, I'll bet you do."

"It's about Egress."

That got his attention. He stopped, turned around, and eyed me from top to toe. A leisurely survey I suffered, letting the bottle dangle, thinking about the fractional application of force that would turn its heavy-bottomed cornglass into a weapon.

His response wasn't what I expected.

His bloodless tongue wet his lips, a dry lizard flicker. "My God, Sarah, what kind of trouble you in?"

It wasn't until I was back out in the Ring, my Projekts protective coloration discarded and my head full of the weird humming that always happens when a job heats up, that I realized what was . . . bothering . . . me.

There were plenty of other agents who wouldn't make a fuss. My psych profile was crystal-clear, I should know. They'd analyzed me twenty ways for each month of my life. Over and over, question after question while I was strapped into the sensachair, my warmbody responses monitored endlessly.

Of course, they wondered about the triggering event. People don't just walk in off the street and request implementation. Oh, you know, sure they do, but I was good material. If I'd been born in the Ring I might have passed some dominance tests and ended up a corporate somebody. My health scan was clean, my legal record fairly spotless, my grades—before I dropped out and went to work running to survive—had been respectable. *Why do you want implementation? What does it mean to you?*

I gave the same answer in a hundred different ways. *I'm tired of being poor. The Projekts are a dead-end street. I heard there are implementation programs where you can work off your debt.* As if I was some starry-eyed idiot who believed you could ever work it off.

I watched the kid's house. The windows were squares of golden light. Rifle would be best, piercing even shock-resistant film, no muss no fuss, I'd be gone before the body hit the ground. Just a shattering and a light thud, painless and easy for him.

Why wasn't I doing it? Why was I thinking, instead, about the past?

It turned out I was a great candidate for full implementation, all my measurements right square in the optimal zone. A doctor in the Free Clinic (hard bitcoin required, no records kept, rejects fallen from Ring grace doing both staff and medical work) had remarked as much, offhand, while he eyed my scan on tempfilm that was already eroding, my feet in the stirrups and the cold probing between my legs. It only took a few minutes before I was scraped empty, cauterized, and out the door. The cramping only lasted an hour.

Why tell the Agency that? Greed, I figured, was an acceptable motive for what I was asking for. The other wasn't their business.

I could have ended up security detail, but I'd been skimmed off the top and slated for delicate Agency work. Erasures mostly, sometimes warnings, sometimes one side or the other of a corporate war when one half—or both—received Agency aid. Even inter-Agency turf wars. Waste of resources, those, but what do I know? I'm just a tool, kept sharp in a drawer and taken out for certain events before dropped back in to wait for the next.

This house, closed up and prim behind its permabrick, was just like every other damn one in its row. Except how many others were sitting on a secret this big?

What was really bothering me? Questions. Just like usual, only this time they weren't the usual ones.

Why, really, would the Agency send *me*? Were they asleep at the switch? My psych profile was unexceptionable even where it detailed my rebellious streak. You couldn't be a good agent without one. Thinking on your feet and solving problems with the required flexibility downright required it. Why me, instead of someone else who didn't have a problem—someone who would probably have found a vantage point and picked him off that very afternoon, right through a window?

Retard. Freak. Scarface.

The offer of a new identity, being quits, or Dismissal.

It was blindingly obvious. Something here stank more that Barlowe's undies.

I slithered down out of the tree, deactivated the camo, and strolled across the street nice and slow. Hands in my pockets, a featureless dark blazer and dungarees, letting the security cams get a good look at me without showing my face or distinguishing features. Subroutines over all my autonomics to keep them nice and even, with quicklocks in case of anything I'd need to alter glandular balance for. I went up the stairs as if I was an old family friend, and didn't press the scanbell. Instead, I knocked, a quick light flurry of taps.

Sometimes people still do that.

There was a pause, a bit too long, and every one of my nerves, implemented and original, twitched.

They weren't expecting me. Someone, stupidly, opened the door.

The male wasn't a problem, he went down as soon as I ripped out his carotid implant. The female came down the stairs in a rush—smell of something red and rich, I kicked the door shut and went down, rolling, as she fired over my head. A blue-white static bolt went overhead with a whoosh, there was a whine of turbo recharge and the chucking of a manipulative re-rack, she had her back to the wall. *"Stay down!"* she yelled, and for a moment I thought she was talking to me.

Through the copper of blood and the scorch of ionization, I could smell her, high emotion pumping out through her warm-body pores. Fear, determination, adrenaline. Familiar.

They all smell the same when the violence starts.

Legs like coiled springs, entire body buzzing with leashed violence. The house was narrow, the stairs came down on the right into the entry hall, kitchen to the back, what was probably a den off to the left, lighted but empty, a stage set. I jackrabbited up—she almost got me, too; I felt the brush of the static bolt. It sizzled past my hip, blasted another hole in the hall wall behind me.

I backhanded her, the greenstick crack of a reinforced but still warmbody neck breaking, and I subtracted the gun from her as she folded down.

When warmbodies go, the sphincters always loosen. It's like the final reminder that in the end, they're all still organic. I didn't know if agents have the same trouble. The nanos are pretty efficient, we can digest just about anything that has any trace nutritive value, plus there's solar and static capability built into our skins nowadays.

I braced the gun. A TekStan static, heavy-duty, if a bolt had hit me I would've had a headache for about ten minutes. I checked the handle—innocent of a corporate logo, but that didn't mean anything. TekStans were like candy, except this one was just on the edge of Agency hardware.

Huh.

I expected screams. Crying. Something, anything. Instead, silence. A single hummingbird heartbeat I could hear—did they have dampers? Secondary security could be up there.

I slid easily, noiselessly, up the stairs. The banister was

odd—metal, a weird resonance. *Entire house could be booby-trapped, but nothing bit at me. Hm. Interesting.*

Padding, small feet on synthsilken carpet. I realized there were no pictures on the walls as I leveled the gun.

He peered out from behind a heavy shockproof door, the edges of its lock-bolts scintillating in the warm golden light from a bloodspattered fixture overhead. How had blood gotten all the way up *there*? Messy, messy.

Huge dark eyes, terribly blank. Was he in shock? I could do this kindly, so quickly he wouldn't feel a thing. If he swung the door closed it would take a while for me to break it.

He didn't. He pushed it open, and stepped out into the hall. His hands fell, pale little birds, to his sides. He was painfully thin, and still in his school uniform. This close I could see a line of grime under each fingernail, and smell . . . what? A dry dusty scent, my scans going a little weird as they tried to pin down what was *off* about him. Even though Sam had told me, I don't suppose I believed it until I got into close scanrange.

Did the other kids feel that instinctive tickle of *something alien*? Was that why the dominant boy had it in for him?

"You're one of *them*." Oddly flat, his little voice. "You're here to kill me."

We stared at each other. The gun, socked against my shoulder, whined with a fresh charge. Just a tiny bit of pressure on the trigger, a gentle squeeze, and flesh would vaporize. If what Sam told me was completely true . . .

"It's okay." That same flat tone, the scar on his chin flushing a little. "I've been expecting it."

I couldn't help myself. "What kind of kid *are* you?"

"I'm an investment." Patiently. "I guess I'm not earning out."

Still staring. I caught a whiff as a random air current moved down the hall. A little dirty, healthy young warmbody, but that weird dry tang. Fear, too. But over it, resignation. The room behind him was a glare of white, and I realized the rich smell downstairs was spaghetti sauce. Stathydroponic tomatoes, to be sure, and weak garlic that had never seen the unveiled sun, but still, it was a rich person's meal.

The kid looked hungry. That room behind him was bare. No posters on the wall, and he hadn't changed into a corporate T-shirt and dungarees, like any other corp kid, from dominant right down to epsilon. I'd bet hard bitcoin he didn't play outside. I'd further bet he didn't have many toys. You'd think they would have enriched his environment, so to speak, but I guess that sort of thing's too expensive nowadays.

His feet were bare, and his toenails curled around the end of his toes. If he was an investment, he hadn't been well taken care of.

Interesting.

I lowered the gun. Its whining was sawing at my nerves. "I don't want to kill you." I even managed to say it like I hadn't maybe decided it right that moment. "If I don't, though, they'll send someone who will."

"I already told you it was okay." Very patiently, as if I was subnormal. "You smell funny. Cyborg, right?"

I nodded. The gun pointed down, loosely. "I don't want to kill you," I repeated, and then I said the most absurd thing I've ever uttered in my entire life. "I want to escape."

Those dark eyes got really big. Geoffrey considered me, the fear struggling in him. I could smell it, sharp and chemical. He was only eight years old. Too young for this sort of thing.

Aren't we all.

"Me too," he said, in a very tiny voice.

Oh, fuck, I thought. *I'm Dismissed for sure.*

* * *

For the first time in years, Sam was late to a meet. I expected as much.

I'd had a lot of time to think, coming back from Cirquit again. There were only a few ways any of this made sense.

Unfortunately, even those few ways ended up with me messily Dismissed. The kid, too. *A practically immortal warmbody*, Sam had told me. *Regenerative organs. Unfortunately it can't transplant, and there are other . . . issues. It requires . . . liquid . . . nutrition.*

No wonder the Agency was involved. Even without transplantive capability, the processes to create this kid could kick implementation right in the teeth.

Sam sat down across from me. This diner, not far from the Projekts—silver and bullet-shaped, its windows filmed with caustic smog and heavy grime—reeked of grease and despair. Dusk filled the street outside, railbuses turning on their forward lamps in deference to archaic laws. It wasn't like it mattered, it was always twilight down under the dome.

I let the silence build. The warmbody waitress—tired mouth, dishwater straggle-hair, and low-grade alloy knee implements—shuffled over.

Sam ordered a cup of sludge. Mine stood in front of me, cooling rapidly. A simple chipped white compressed-clay mug, probably older than me. Maybe even older than Sam. It was a miracle it hadn't broken by now.

When I looked up, he was studying my face. We were both flatline, and his hands rested in plain sight on the tabletop. So did mine.

"It's done," I said, evenly. *"Confirmed kill."*

He actually turned paler, if only fractionally. His autonomics were probably struggling something fierce. I glanced over his shoulder. The waitress had vanished into the steam-heat of the kitchen, despite the sludgepot bubbling right on the counter. *Ah.*

He blinked. As tells went, it wasn't a huge one, but then, when you've sat across from someone for years, getting your marching orders, it doesn't have to be.

I was over the table, my hand cramping as I shoved the sharp point of the shivprobe between two strong flexible ribs, my other hand wrenching his head aside with a screech. It sounds different than breaking a warmbody's cervical spine, stresses going up into high harmonics. Precision of force is needed, to fracture it *just* right.

His body bucked and crackled, static overwhelming subroutines, paralyzing systems. He did still have implanted Dismissal switches, they popped and fused just like Barlowe said they would with the palm-activator he'd given me, slapped against Sam's bare skin.

Bet that's uncomfortable. I pitched aside, rolling, as the windows cracked and shattered under a hail of static and projectile fire.

Dragging a twitching agent along a filthy diner floor while security troops—mostly warmbody, since I could hear audible chatter—is not a lot of fun. It was better than being caught in the barrage the instant someone outside guessed I wasn't quite as easily led as they *thought* I was.

Corporation. Maybe Niful. This didn't come from Control. Or is the Agency hand in glove with a corp for this experiment? Turf battle? No, too public.

Someone's fingers were going to get singed over this. If Sam was running on the side . . . but *why*? And why pick me? I'd never turned down a mission, threatening me with Dismissal wasn't necessary . . .

. . . unless he wanted me pissed off enough to *not* kill the kid. Maybe he'd been banking on it?

Didn't matter at the moment. The kitchen was deserted.

Automations whined, dishwashing and steamjets going full-bore. *Distractions, and cover.* There was a door to the alley, I tossed Sam's weight out first with a sickening crack as they blew in through the front of the diner. Sounded like a rocket, probably ArGen tech. Could mean nothing.

Get moving. I tossed Barlowe's other present—wasn't he a giving soul?—behind me. Followed Sam's heavy, limp body, an uncontrolled jump that ended with me on top of him, rolling as projectile fire spattered the concrete behind me. The lumps of dead warmbody near the refuse containers were probably the diner's staff, and the waitress's fatigued legs were forever still now. Maybe she'd thought it was a police action, maybe she even believed they would keep her safe.

I dumped my still-twitching burden safely behind said rubbish bins, snapping the silicacine cuffs over his wrists and sticking the gag in. Barlowe said any agent would be out until I took the sharp shivprobe through the chest away, but no use in being less than thorough. That done, I whirled, my camo fizzing as they switched to static bolts. The detonation of Barlowe's toy behind me was an EMP pulse. It would fuzz their scopes and oculars something fierce, but mine were buffered.

A momentary scan pinpointed heartbeats quickened with excitement, sweat with adrenaline tang, whistling breaths. Some of them had autonomic implants, but the control isn't perfect. Not even close.

Not like an agent's.

Time to hunt.

"The body?" Barlowe wanted to know.

I dumped the contents of Sam's pockets onto the glass counter. "Dropped in a vat of IcarenCorp chemsludge. It will give us a few hours before they fish him out and start asking questions. They may even think he's me for a little bit." I let my fingers travel over the assorted odds and ends. "See? Identicard, a plasma impress . . . He expected me to bring the kid, or tell him where he was. Idiot."

"No." Barlowe eyed me, his ocular glinting for a moment. "I would've expected it too. You don't have the childkiller look, Sarah."

I shrugged.

"Abby?" A piping little cry. "Abby?"

I controlled a flinch. Geoff appeared, slightly damp—looked like Barlowe had run him through a chemshower. He'd also found the kid some clothes. With a blue long-sleeved RebeCorp T-shirt, dungarees and boots held together by a judicious application of stat-tape, he looked a lot more normal.

But those eyes. They would give the game away, even to another warmbody. If, and only if, they cared enough to look.

Geoff ran around the end of the counter and flung his arms around me. Clinging for dear life, I guess. "You came back!"

"I said I would." I tried not to sound irritated. Barlowe's eyebrows, such as they were, had risen to dangerous heights. "We can't stay here without bringing them down on you. They might find you anyway."

Barlowe waved a horny, callused hand. "I'll be somewhere else. I'll even look different." A pause. "About Egress."

"What about it?" I was raw all over. That made twice I'd almost gone at the old man. I kept expecting—maybe even hoping for—a betrayal, Barlowe thinking he had a good chance to make some cash. Someone wanted this kid, bad.

Of course they did, he was worth a lot. His organs might be regenerative; even if he wasn't useful for replacing worn out corp exec's warmbody failings he'd make a fine soldier.

Why did they have him stashed in that bare, sterile house? Perfect cover, but no place for a kid.

Did it matter? When a corporation controls you, it's not an enlightened despot. You're fungible. I hunched my shoulders, trying not to feel terribly exposed. A lot depended on the next few minutes.

Barlowe poked through the piles on the countertop. Blue neon fizzed outside. "This will get you through Station. You'll have to figure out how to break out of the train in the Waste. You sure you want to do that?"

"Another City will be just as bad as this one." I shrugged. "Get out from broadcast range for killcodes, scavenge enough tech to . . . I don't know. There's settlements. Some of them might not even be completely owned."

"Optimist." Barlowe made a few of the bits on the counter vanish. I'd brought him little shards of Facilitator kit he could sell, too. They would be hot, and they wouldn't last long, but if anyone could turn a profit on them, he could. They lulled any suspicion he might have. "Next you'll be telling me you believe in Nikor's Rebels."

You don't know what I believe. I glanced down at Geoff. Figuring out how to get him what he needed to . . . eat . . . was going to be difficult at best. "I'm as clear from Dismiss implants as you can make me, right?"

"You've been clear for a while now. I take pride in my work." Barlowe grumbled a bit more. He reached over the counter, motioning for Geoff to press his thumb on the plasma impress. "So, Sarah . . . any last request?"

The kid glanced at me, and when I nodded he licked his thumb and made a good stamp. It sealed onto the fresh identicard, and I did the other one. Two brand-spanking-new passes with nice safe code on them. I slipped both in my pocket. "Got a coat for the kid?" Thankfully, the bead curtain had stopped clashing and slithering behind me.

"He does," Geoff piped up. "I'll get it." He was gone behind the counter like a shot.

I was glad. I didn't want him to see what happened next.

Still, when he came out, very slowly, clutching a ratty parka two sizes too big for him, I didn't care for the look on his face.

"They would find him," I managed, a bit lamely. "And you . . . you need to . . . drink."

Geoff's mouth was slightly open. The tiny sharp points of his canines showed, and any idiot could see they were subtly modified. The scar wasn't surgical, the flesh separated naturally so the jaw could crack wide and get good purchase.

"He's fresh." I sounded harsh even to myself. "Don't waste it."

Barlowe's body twitched, too, when Geoff sank his small fangs into its wrist. I held him there, a railprobe right through the old man's forehead, and listened to the sucking sounds.

He was quiet until the train's doors closed. I was turning over the problem of how to get *off* a sealed train in the middle of a wilderness inside my mostly-invulnerable skull.

Geoff sat between me and the wall. "Your name's not Abby."

I heard trains once had windows, before the Cities sealed up and Egress became a dirty word. Everyone on a train keeps their distance. There were only five in this sixteen-seater compartment, and if we kept it down, none of the others would hear us over the noise of repellers waking up and gears grinding.

I settled into stillness. We weren't past the walls yet.

The Waste was either a radioactive desert or a lush Eden swarming with flesh-eating insects and brain-fried cannibal rebels. At least, so they told us in school.

Right now I had my doubts, and I hoped they were good enough.

"It is now," I answered, finally. *Names don't matter. Not for me.*

"Why did you do that? He was nice. He wanted to help."

"I told you, they would have found him. That's what they *do*, the people I thought I was working for. The people who made me." *And believe me, this was cleaner than what they'd do to him.*

The identicards had gotten us this far. Had Sam been thinking he would flee with the kid? Was he working for another City? Corporations were largely interCity; the Agency has offices in every hub, of course. Sam might have been expecting a warm welcome somewhere else. I'd probably never know.

Geoff was silent. Why did it sting? Why was I also feeling the need to *explain* myself? "You wanted to escape. We're going to. I had to kill him, kid." *Aren't you grateful? You should be.*

I wasn't being exactly fair. He probably didn't know if I'd take care of him as a proper investment . . . or not.

The lights dimmed, the train jerked forward. When I derailed it I'd have to scavenge through the cargo cars for anything useful.

"Are you gonna kill me now?" Very quiet. I caught a breath—copper, fear and whatever lingered in his mouth from his meal. He was looking a little rosier, but that could have been the dim light. If there weren't mammals out in the Waste he could survive on I was going to either have to think of something else or watch him starve to death.

I'll find something. I have to. "Of course not. What do you think I am?" I thought about the doctor, and the sucking sound as tech pulled a bundle of multiplying cells out of me. My feet in the stirrups, and the cold. *Why do you want implementation, Miss?*

Another long pause. Then, surprising me, his small fingers—so fragile, so easy to hurt—threaded between mine, lying discarded on the armrest. He squeezed, almost painfully hard, and I was very gentle.

"Mom?" he said, testing the word.

For the second time, an audible laugh caught me by surprise. The sound of the train gathering itself as it lurched out of Station covered the noise. "I'm not the maternal type, kid."

The stench of the lavatory behind us was why nobody had chosen this pair of seats, but I could shut off that band of nasal receptors. He probably couldn't, but he didn't complain.

"That's okay." There it was again, the wistfulness. "I'm not a real kid."

I took a deep breath. Another. The scraping inside me, and my own fierce determination a sourness in my warmbody mouth. A baby in the Projekts was an anchor, and runners needed to be light and fast. The cash I'd skimmed from several shipments was spent to cut and cauterize the deadweight away, and knowing they would catch me when the accounts didn't balance. There was a way out, in a doctor's chance observation, instead of the desperate jumping around I'd been working over and over inside my warmbody skull.

Bright white light, the cold, and the hideous cramping that only lasted an hour. Eight years ago. Funny, that.

"Yes, you are." I had to work to make the words audible. There was an obstruction in my throat, even though all my autonomics were flatline. "You're *my* kid, now. Better be quiet and rest." I glanced over the interior of the car again, and a plan began to form.

He didn't take his hand away. I didn't take mine away either.

"We've got a long way to go," I told him, and held his fingers as the train slid through the City's walls.

CHAPTER ONE

SEALED TRAIN

"I told you, a wolf's head can still bite."

—*Lady Iboshi,* Princess Mononoke

I thought derailing—or just plain getting *off*—a sealed train in the middle of the Waste would be difficult, but not impossible. Otherwise I might have been reduced to commandeering a corporate thopter somehow, and though "agent" means "theoretically invulnerable," the idea of a crash from that height, smoking and twisted wreckage, and being tracked by *other* thopters while on foot and carrying a maybe-damaged kid wasn't pleasant in the least. As it was, all I had to worry about was when to start moving, and how to keep said kid from being splattered all over the landscape when we leapt from something going as fast as an interCity magtrain.

Geoff dozed next to me, rosy-cheeked even in the dim glow from cheap redscreen bulbs, canned air soughing over us both. This close, the pearly glimmer of his teeth was even more startlingly alien. They were shaped differently, like his cheekbones, and the thick vertical scar on his chin looked surgical.

It wasn't.

Still, our costumes were pretty perfect—Geoff's ratty parka a shade too big for him, a blue, long-sleeved Static Rebe T-shirt, dungarees, and judicious amounts of stat tape reinforcing his boots; me in a tailored plasleather jacket with plenty of pockets and dungarees just a little too designer to be plebe but not designer enough to be high corporate power. We sat quietly, the very picture of single mother locked into low-level corporate servitude by her Special Needs brat but smart and vicious enough to both keep the kid and qualify for travel privileges. The observant onlooker would think *courier*, and if they were innocent, that would be the end of it.

If they weren't, they'd be looking for my cargo. Funny how this was my protective coloration—courier was how I'd started out, long ago, a runner dodging bullets and static-bolt ammo in the Projekts.

Before I was implemented. Before I was *agent*.

Our five fellow passengers hadn't moved much since the train jolted out through stat-veiled clockwork gates and into the inimical wasteland outside the cities. Cannibals, flesh-eating plants, and radioactive sludge creating massive hideous beasts were supposed to be the reasons for sealing every City and every Egress Train. Some quasi-rebels—creeping in corners, holding muttered meetings in fauxsmoke-filled bars—inside the walls whispered that if we knew what was really outside the walls, we wouldn't stay in the perpetual twilight, under smoggy or UV-domed skies with the weight of every breath owned by one corporation or another.

We were going to take our chances. I was just hoping Geoff could live off any mammal, or that we'd find enough relatively healthy cannibals for him to get what he needed. The prospect of radiation poisoning worried me, but there was only so much I could do about it.

The subroutines over my autonomics kept clamping down, and I had to pop another one over my glandular balance to stop the cortisol and adrenaline from swamping me. It wasn't a good time to start getting jitters, only two and a half hours out of the gate. I kept staring at the front of the carriage we were in, blinking every so often, turning everything over inside my head, searching for the missing piece.

It bothered me. No, not Barlowe's body hanging from a rail-probe—that fell under the rubric of "necessary casualty," not to mention "insurance." It was a cleaner death than any corporation or the Agency would have given him, too.

Also on the did-not-bother-me list: pieces of my handler dumped in a vat of caustic sludge. They would fish Sam out, clean him up, and he'd have a lot of explaining to do, both to the Agency and to the corporation looking to reclaim Geoff. Unless Sam had a helluva good story and a reason to use it, the Agency would start digging; in a little while they would come after me to recoup their investment in my implementations, or to just-plain-Dismiss me as a bad loss.

It was only a matter of time, but I'd take all I could get. *That* didn't bother me either. Well, not much. About as much as the likely bacterial content on the thin nyla-covered cushion underneath me, which had soaked up who-knew-what from however many warmbodies. There used to be a lot more traffic between Cities before the big transports went airborne.

No, what was bothering me was the house I'd found Geoff in. His white bedroom too bare, and the corporate bodyguards acting as "parents" too neglectful. On the other hand, the kid was . . . different. His facial structure was off by a few millimeters, or maybe it was his expression. That scar on his chin, the set of his thin shoulders, and his eerie stillness made normals . . . uncomfortable. Like the other kids at his school, although they could have been responding to his general air of disrepair.

Kids can smell when one of their own is already weak. Humans: perfect predators before they're socialized. Then they mostly get old and tired.

Not always, though. Some of them keep that perfection all the way to the grave.

The kid twitched, waking from his doze. "Abby?"

It's an okay name, I told myself, wishing I hadn't given it to him. I was stuck with it now. "What?"

"Where are we going?"

You didn't ask earlier. "Out."

He still hadn't left go of my right hand. No longer tentative, he sometimes squeezed, and I surprised myself by squeezing back, but very gently. Such a small hand, and he was running warm now. Slightly above 38C, as if he had a low-grade fever. His galvanic skin response was fine, though, and the rest of him seemed okay to my scans, despite its slight differences from warmbody norms. They weren't *obvious, glaring* variances. Whoever had designed him had done a good job.

"Then where?" he whispered. Big dark eyes in that wan face, like a holo of a genegrown puppy on an advert for candies or skinshield.

I was about to tell him I didn't know, that I'd figure something out, when the train lurched crazily. Stress-harmonics went up into ultrasonic, sending a spike of pain through my head before a reflexive filter dropped into place over that intake channel, and my arm was a bar of solid steel diagonally across Geoff's chest, bracing him into the seat as I dug my heels in against sudden deceleration.

The train had stopped, but everything inside it was still going.

Physics is a cold, heartless bitch. Geoff folded forward around my arm, just like a spider flicked into a static seal-field. At least he wasn't in freefall across the carriage, but if he ended up with whiplash or internal bleeding I was going to have to get creative with my field-medical training.

The back of the carriage lifted high, the car behind us doing its best to keep humming along the tracks. Squeals of tortured metal, crunching and snapping sounds, a sharp stink from the lavatory. Geoff's piping little cry as air was forced out of his lungs, but I'd already broken the force of the deceleration enough for him to stay put, clinging to his seat, and was on my feet as the entire carriage tilted crazily. The stress-sounds were highest along one of the welded seams, and the buckling floor had popped up one end of a bench seat. A quick strike to break the seatback free, then my fingers curled around the horizontal support bar under the nylacushions, the patient bearer of so many asses, now torn free with a shriek lost in the general chaos. Crumpled bodies—someone had lost control of their bowels, the common warmbody response to sudden trauma.

Everyone shits when death comes calling. Except agents, because the colony of nanos we carry is too efficient at stripping anything we ingest of any nutritive value and using every scrap.

Move. Now I had a metal bar that would have to serve as both tool and weapon. I arrived in front of Geoff, who flinched at my sudden blinking through space too fast for warmbody eyes to track—but his gaze had stayed unerringly on me all through the split-seconds, with more-than-human accuracy. Perched up in our seats, now high on a buckled mountain of metal, he wrapped his arms around his middle and stared. I hefted the bar experimentally as a sliver of rancid golden light speared the dim red-lit hell that had been a train carriage hauling a sparse contingent of losers from one City-warren to the next.

Yet another reason I'd chosen the seats back here—any

sudden magtrain problem of enough severity tends to accordion the cars, and they bust like overripe stathydroponic fruit.

Screaming. The distant rumbling of explosions—a fuel core had been breached, by the sound of it. I filtered that out, because under the chaos was another noise—the snap-crackle of static-bolt rifles, the pop and ping of projectile ammo from handhelds.

Looked like I was saved the trouble of derailing or bursting a welded seam. Now I was a lone agent with a chunk of subpar metal and a big-eyed kid to protect.

I got to work.

Dust. More screaming, and a narrow band-frequency around us was suddenly alive with commchatter. I popped a subroutine on that intake feed, standard record-and-flag, and swung the bar one last time. The warmbodies largely didn't know what hit them. Dazed by the sudden crash, some with broken bones, I caved in their skulls like hydroponic plasma bags. Splatters of blood and brainmatter, glints as chips fell free—two of them were standard-issue implemented, probably secretaries with subvocals and recording capability. I tore the throatboxes out of both and crushed them, just to make sure.

Geoff, trembling, clung to his tilted-forward seat even though a tide of nasty blue chemwash flooded downhill from the lavatories. At least the organic matter wasn't crawling with bacteria, but the smell was horrific and I wasn't filtering out my nasals anymore, I needed all the information I could get. I hopped up the few still-bolted seats to avoid the slippery bits just as shadows filled the crack torn in the side of the car.

Shit. Thought I had more time. "Come on," I mouthed, and Geoff scrambled to obey. He went on my back, arms and legs locking around me, and I had to adjust his grip around my throat a little ungently. It was hard to turn my head, but I'd switched to panoptics anyway. The shaking going through him was worrisome.

So was the idea that he might think I'd've been coming up the car to pop his skull, too, instead of just cleaning up anyone who could possibly remember us. It would be a natural response on his part.

The irony of expecting anything resembling natural response from this corp-created kid wasn't lost on me, but I had no time to think about it because the sputter and hiss of stat-fueled cutters sent a red spike through all my intakes, and my skin roughened before I brought the response back down to precombat levels, saving all my energy for a sudden burst of frenetic motion. The crack widened, superheated metal singing as it separated, widening the hole.

"Six." Geoff's hot breath on my ear, under my tangled dark hair. "I can hear them."

I didn't waste respiration telling him I did too, and that he'd missed one. Six heartbeats, popping along high and hard, none of them implemented beyond some basic combat reinforcement—and shoddy, sloppy work of it, too, if my ears weren't deceiving me.

The seventh pulse was as steady and calm as my own, and semi-buffered as well.

It was another agent.

The first place a sweep team looks is down. Inescapable human habit, searching the ground you're going to be stepping on. Besides, the crack in the side of the train, added to the slope created when the car behind us wedged underneath this one, made it logical to assume everything would be jumbled at the bottom. The last thing they probably expected was an agent clinging to the ceiling, wedged in a tangle of metal and tough fabric netting that had disgorged its cargo of baggage onto the floor in the first jolt. Most of the injuries to our fellow passengers had been from those sudden missiles.

Well, except for the ones I'd inflicted.

I dropped into the middle of them and broke two immediately, swinging the bar laterally to crush ribs and get them out of the way. A snap-kick to the leader's knee to put him down—he reeked of dominance and cheap harsh liquor, his head a mass of wild dark sand-grimed hair stuck with feathers and bits of circuit wire glinting as he dropped. Smears of some kind of paint on their faces, red and chalk-white, their gear bits and bobs cobbled together—looked scavenged—and I was revising my initial dread that they were a capture team sent from in-City.

Which meant I probably shouldn't have bothered to put Geoff on my back where I could be reasonably sure nobody would snatch him. Like they say, hindsight has panoptics.

Get them down, where's that fucking agent? Where? You don't strike where you think we might be, or where you expect us to be—you have to anticipate, outthink, and hit where we *are.*

In this case, though, my opponent was transport-slow and sloppy. Of course, tagging along with train-hunting cannibals in the Waste might do that to you. And only semi-buffered? Maybe an older implementation?

Thud. Agent on the roof. An instinctive leap to get the high ground, or part of a plan? No time, I was already past the clot of warmbodies dead or still mostly breathing, with their piecemeal implements and augments. The metal in my hands was too soft to crack an agent's reinforced ribcage, and there was no way I could cause enough internal damage to put him down quickly enough. So, that left just one option, and I had to do it with Geoff clinging to my back.

The glare burst through my eyes, scoring into my skull as I burst out and took my first breath of non-mineralized, unsmoggy out-City air. Geoff let out a high piping fear-cry but I was already twisting, one hand curled around a support strut and the rest of my body whipping as force transferred, the kid's arms and legs clamping down and cutting off my oxygen as he struggled to stay aboard. Blinded, clumsy because of the extra weight and the need to go less-than-quarter-speed so he wouldn't be flung off into space, it was with more brute force than skill that I landed correctly on the crumpled, steaming metal lid of the car. Whirling, my bootheels scraping for purchase, and the shock of a blow to my belly—*dammit, he hit me, too slow*—as I rammed into the other agent.

You get even a bar of soft metal moving quickly enough, and you can pierce the weaker spots alongside the throatbox. Crunching, levering the bar as the other agent screamed—high male noise, spray of blood laced with silver motes of nanos very much like my own—and a sudden loss of blood pressure from the shiv dragged across my stomach threatened to drop me before I could wrench the other agent's head off his reinforced neck, shearing the cervicals *just* right. The feedback squeal cut out and I crumpled, my shredded midriff a hot bar of pain. Coughing, a burst of fluid from my abused lungs and stomach, the nanos swarming and patching. Damage critical but there was glorious raw unfiltered sunlight nailing us to the top of the roof, flooding my suddenly darkening skin with the power needed for repair. Geoff screaming some more and I tumbled off the roof with the other agent's head in my fist, dangling bits of meat and reinforced cervical structures. The body was still thumping around up top, nerves scrabbling blindly against the shock. The nanos would seal everything up and keep it in stasis until the cervicals got within reach of each other, then they would meld and he'd be good as new.

At least, until the nanos exhausted every molecule of nutriment stored in his tissues, or the body ran out of solar charge.

Right now, though, I swung the head, cracking one of the remaining warmbodies across his un-reinforced skull. Burst of brain and blood and bone, the gloom of the car interior just as stunning as the nuclear glow outside. Geoff slid free of my back, still screeching, and I had seconds to deal with the last two ambulatory attackers.

Plenty of time.

Two cracks and soft thumps, and the only sound was the leader's heavy desperate breathing as he scrabbled for his pistol, an antique projectile number. I knocked it away with a clatter, probably breaking his finger in the process, and crouched, dangling the agent's head—heavy, a hell of a flail—from my left hand, my fist wrapped in long dark hair with scratchy circuit wire threaded through. Adornment, that perennial human need, ranking right after food and shelter. "Geoff?"

"Bright," the kid gasped, but he didn't sound any worse than just-breathless. "Couldn't hold on. Sorry."

"It's all right. Come here."

The leader swore at me, vile anatomically-impossible terms in an accent far away from City Spanics. A drawl tangled and tainted his vocals, and I kept the record-and-flag going. Always helpful to talk like the locals, a lesson left over from agent training.

Geoff crept painfully up the slick, tilted. His boots didn't slip, because he placed them with such tentative care. "What are you going to do?" Hitching and unsteady, as if he feared punishment. The leader swore at me again, adrenaline and pain soaking his glandular wash.

I sighed. My own hormonal balance had spiked up for combat, and it was more difficult than I liked to bring it down.

The commchatter had faded into the crackle of live lines open but nobody talking. A seven-man team to derail a whole train? It didn't seem credible, but then, they had an agent.

Operative word there, *had.* If not for the sudden flood of solar, and the fact that I was a flex liquidator and knew just the right angle and force to apply to shear even reinforced cervicals, *had* might have been my operative word too.

"You." I waved the head a little, to get the leader's attention. "Any more in your team? Anyone outside?"

He spat at me. The wad of thick phlegm splatted against my cheek, and the reflexive chemtesting in my skin didn't catch the expected tang. None of the markers of Adison's ketosis, the body rebelling at eating human proteins.

Huh. Might not be a cannibal. In any case, the sudden lack of commchatter told me we were clear enough.

For now.

I turned my head slightly so my panoptics, adjusted now to both the golden hammerlight outside and the red emergency-lit dimness in here, could take Geoff in. His hair was a wild mess, but he looked otherwise all right. He blinked several times, and under the various nasty smells collected in this little car, the copper of blood suddenly became noticeable.

"How bad are you hurt?" He scanned fine, but contusions would take a few minutes to show.

"Not bad. Abby, Mom . . . I'm . . . I'm thirsty." Whispered, barely audible under the leader's fresh ranting tumble of obscenities.

I dropped the head and darted forward, breaking the leader's right arm, then braced myself and lifted him by the throat. Applied just enough pressure to the carotid, and the sudden blissful silence was a balm. "I know, kid. I left this one alive for you. He's disease-free, come and get it."

Geoff crept forward, a stray's cringing.

"It's okay," I soothed. "It's just fine, kiddo. Come on." *Just get it over with, please.* "What did they feed you before?"

"Cloned." He cleared his throat, then came the small sound of the scar on his chin separating and his jaw distending, familiar from Barlowe's suspended home in the Cirquit. The unconscious body I held twitched a little as Geoff sank his teeth in, and the gulping began.

He drank his fill.

The cars in front of us were crumpled between walls of relatively soft red rock rising on either side of a gorge, tall spiny plants and other crowding succulents clinging in the cracks and a merciless pale-blue sky hung overhead on a single golden nail. A pall of greasy blue fuelcore smoke lifted from the very head of the train, the engine shredded to a fare-thee-well. I wondered how they did it until I smelled the caustic reek of altahan, probably mixed up from City sludge and outlying refuse dumps. Spark a fuse as a magtrain thunders down a track, judging the few seconds of lead time it needed to develop *just* right, and you had a reaction that would shatter fuelcores as it broke the sound barrier. Cheap, nasty, and extremely effective.

I'd have to keep it in mind if I had to begin cracking and stripping trains to feed both of us.

The cars behind us had few survivors, and they were stunned and easily taken care of. No witnesses, nothing to slow us down.

I scavenged medkits and clothing while keeping an ear tuned to both audible and comms. The driver AI could have been crippled into losing contact, or down here in a gully all the attackers had to do was sabotage one relay station right before they hit the tracks and the train might show up as malfunctioning instead of dead and opened like a can of protein shake. I dragged the entry team's bodies out, weighing the advisability of just making them vanish, while Geoff huddled in the dim, malodorous shelter of our carriage.

The light hurt him, and it was the safest place for a noncombatant anyway.

In the end, I decided distance was better than taking the time to leave a mystery for the cleanup crews. When I slid back in through the hole in the side of the carriage, I found the boy rocking back and forth on a seat that had wedged itself against the wall, hugging himself. His elbows were sharp points, even through the parka.

"Here. We'll wrap you up." I shrugged out of the pack and looked for a dry spot to set the pile of stripped and scavenged clothing. The attackers had some usable gear—piecemeal like everything else they carried, but the agent didn't have any Agency kit. I didn't quite like that, but if it meant they weren't a capture team I could live with it. Besides, if he was only partially buffered, he was almost certainly older. Nowadays the buffering adapts to every new field it encountered, except plas.

Always excepting the plas.

"It's so bright." He shuddered, hugging himself. "It wasn't like that at home."

"Cities have UV domes. The statrepellers fuel them. You okay?"

"I . . . I think so. You killed them all."

"I did." I held up pair of tinted goggles taken from the smallest of the attackers. With a little modification, they would fit his kid-sized head. "Think you can wear these?"

"Why did you kill them?"

It surprised me. Asking *why*. He'd asked about Barlowe, too. "No witnesses, no deadweight. I can't haul survivors around, and can't leave them for questioning. Not that the Agency won't suspect, especially when they . . . anyway, the more ambiguity, the better."

"Deadweight." He still hugged himself, and his eyes were cat-gleams in the dark. "Are you . . . am I deadweight too?"

Maybe he didn't even know what he was wondering. Maybe he didn't want to say it out loud. "Of course not. You're *my* kid, Geoff." *And I want to live. Which means you have to.*

That seemed to reassure him. At least, he stopped shaking so badly. I waited, impatience ticking under my skin, while he absorbed the information. "So . . . you *are* my mom?"

Oh, for fucksake. "I am *now*. Come on, we need to get out of here. Sooner or later they'll send thopters to check this piece of track. We need to be far away when that happens."

CHAPTER TWO

CANNIBAL WARFARE

We marched into a heat-haze afternoon, the horizon shimmering with false promise, and stacks of that reddish rock occasionally breaking a sea of deceptively gentle sand-waves. Geoff didn't complain, even when the sunlight worked through the wrappings and raised blistering weals on pale skin. He would have gone until he dropped from the fourpad's broad back and cracked his head on a rock, if I hadn't been paying attention.

We weren't far enough away, not by a long shot. Tracking the would-be train robbers to their supplies turned out to be child's play, and the shaggy creatures with broad padded feet we found there were docile enough. All sorts of usable gear hung off each big, hairy, smelly beast, there were ropes to keep them tethered, and their long split-lipped faces and mournful veiled dark eyes were familiar from holos and old books escaped into dusty forgotten corners.

Basic literacy was about all public edu could give you, if a corporation wanted more they'd train you, and most Projekts kids dropped out early. But *drop out of school* doesn't mean *stop paying attention*, because even a poor kid from the Projekts can figure out that staying brainsharp keeps you going a lot longer than expensive augments or xaco-laced protein shakes. Most runners freelancing for the drug lords don't survive past eighteen. You found another line of work or you died, it was that simple.

If Geoff needed more . . . fluids . . . we'd have to see if any mammal would do. At least these potential meals carried their own weight.

Geoff swayed atop his fourpad when we stopped, and I landed with an ungraceful thud. Riding the beasts was bad enough, between the awkward motion and the constant refining of muscular algorithms, but it was probably the heat that sapped him.

Or the multiple traumas of the last couple days. Death, destruction, fearing for his own survival, and come to think of it, I wasn't a cuddly type.

Agents never are.

He half-fell into my arms; I hugged him close despite the heat. "Shit. Why didn't you say something?"

"Deadweight," he murmured through chapped lips under a thin bandanna.

Those towers of rock broke the sandy, simmering soil all around us, and the thick spine-quivering plants massed wherever there was shade didn't look welcoming. Nevertheless, my area scan picked up all sorts of interesting movements out of the sunglare. There was life here, burrowing deep to escape the suffocating heat. A deeper scan, my eyes closed while other senses sent out concentric rings of awareness, came up with a couple options, none of them very good.

At least there were shallow caves in the rock towers. One of them was large enough to shade us and the fourpads, who wandered over to the jagged, spike-leaved plants and began cropping at them enthusiastically. As soon as we were in the relatively cooler shade, Geoff perked up a little, and one of the full-sloshing canteens that held water instead of eyewatering-strong, clear alcohol held to his mouth produced a response. He drank—but not greedily, without gulping, and behind the goggles his eyes were half-lidded.

"That's right," I found myself saying. "It's okay, kid. Next time say something, okay?"

He didn't reply. I propped him against the sandstone wall, carefully, and unwrapped his head. That was when I saw the blisters. *Huh. Those look nasty.*

"You're probably sensitive to UV," I continued. "But those blisters look odd." Why was I blathering like an idiot instead of getting the fourpads situated? "Stay here, and drink some more water, but slowly." I unbuckled the goggles and loosened his scarf, and he nodded, dozily. The vesicles and rashes were already shrinking, the flush in his cheeks from his . . . meal . . . smoothing them away.

Thought-provoking, indeed. That kind of healing without implementation, without the nanos, was impossible. It was why we had nanos to begin with. Everything about Geoff flew in the face of the science that had built me.

Well, maybe not *built* me, but certainly *remade* me. I'd been a perfect candidate for implementation, all my measurements smack dab in the middle of optimal ranges, but I might have died a runner's death at seventeen except for the bad luck getting caught by a flashgang of rival runners at the station between Cheska and the edge of the Projekts.

Shake it off, agent. After all, we were outside the Cities now. I didn't have to replay any memory I didn't care to.

I want to escape, I'd said, pointing a rifle at a big-eyed kid I'd been told to kill. Well, here we were. The persistent feeling of missing something, of some vital piece of the puzzle invisible from my angle, was too nagging to be nervousness. Maybe I was sloppy, one shock after another overwhelming even an agent's flexibility and capacity.

I hoped not.

I had to figure out how to keep the fourpads from running off, and make sure they would stay out of the sun. They were eating the spiny bushes down to nubs, and seemed just fine. With that done, I could turn my attention to preparing the cave for the next few hours. Once dusk hit, we'd have to move again.

Except Geoff was asleep, curled on his side with his thumb in his mouth, as if he was five instead of eight. I crouched for a little while on the other side of the cavern, watching.

I'm an investment, he'd told me, calmly. *I guess I'm not earning out.* It wasn't so much hearing it in a kid's clear little voice, because by his age I'd known all about profit and loss and investments too. When the corporations own everything, it's a lesson you get early, and deep.

It was suddenly hearing how *wrong* it sounded.

Maybe I was having an ethics crisis, but if anything in my psych profile had pointed toward that kind of handicap the Agency would have Dismissed me early, either with an explosive switch implanted somewhere in the standard agent upgrades or the old-fashioned way, like the head stuffed in one of the saddlebags. Finding a good place to drop it off was lower on my list of priorities than keeping my kid alive.

He needed rest.

I sighed, my internals dialed into the red for no good reason at all. My hormone balance was wonky, and even with the flush of solar—the nanos turning my skin into one giant mouth greedily gulping at that nuclear shower of free energy—I felt . . . tired.

Empty. I never thought I'd miss the whitenoise of hovers and statrepellers, the constant heaving background surfroar of crowds shuffling along, tenements stacked high with cubes rented per week or month, the buzzing of holo adverts and the blinking of LED displays enticing you to spend, spend, spend. The waves of stat-bolts and flying ammo passing overhead, the subliminal hum of chatter on every band that could possibly hold it, most of it encrypted, the noise as machines underground cycled through recycling water and organic matter into different forms to keep the warren full of ants seething along.

Out here, there was only the wind, a faint breeze that did more harm than good, because water loss would turn you into dried meat before long. The fourpads could pinch their nostrils shut and lid their eyes, and they didn't seem to be in too much danger of dehydration if they could eat the greenery.

So this was the Waste, and we were alone. Just me and the dozing, fragile baggage I'd thrown my entire career, life, *existence* away for.

I took a few deep breaths, my hormone balance evening out slowly, and got back to the job of ensuring our survival.

Geoff woke with a jerk when the fire crackled. Dusk proved to be the best time to hunt, since things started waking up, and I was pleasantly surprised by the Waste not being a radioactive hell stripped bare of everything that could support life. Not a lot of water, but the spiny bushes had long flat leaves buried under the spikes that the fourpads sucked on, and *those* were full of moisture. The other succulents were good for that too, except for some purple ones the fourpads avoided; testing the helixes showed me the cute little tempting buttons were full of alkaloid poisons.

It beggared belief how anything could live out here, but

tenacity always wins. Three little furry things had gotten too close to my inhuman stillness, thinking me a part of the landscape, and paid for it with swift neck-cracking death. They were soft, brown-furred, and had long high pointed ears, and I was irrationally glad Geoff hadn't seen me gutting them. At least I knew to get the offal out and away, mostly because I'd read a comic once about the aftermath of the Sidon Incident and the Gene Wars sweeping the entire planet's surface. Sometimes people said there were mutated leftovers from that time living in the wastelands along with the cannibals, and that they'd saved John Nikor however-many years ago when he'd busted out of CranCorp's City-chain to the east and started the whole settlements-and-townships thing.

Of course I'd thought about it. Who hasn't heard of Libera, and Nikor's Rebellion? Libera can be anything you want it to be, when you're tired of corporations bleeding you dry. You believe in someone, somewhere, who isn't bought and sold.

Someone who isn't *owned*.

Geoff stretched, yawning, and pushed himself up to sit. The fire painted his face a warm gold, and the static cells I'd rigged across the cave's entrance crackled the smoke into a fine ash that drifted down in bursts as it collected. The little animals roasting in our tiny blaze were probably going to be charred outside and raw inside, but they were better than nothing.

"Abby?" He swallowed, hard. "Mom?"

"I'm here." I pointed at the back of the cave. "If you need to eliminate do it back there. Things get active here after dark." *Last thing you need is to get bitten on the ass by something venomous.*

"Oh." He rubbed at his eyes, and for a moment I was years in the past, back in the City, looking out a grime-darkened window at the points of light in other tenement windows, hearing the waves of flying ammunition go overhead as wars were fought for rooftop vantages. My hand over my belly, below my umbilical dimple, fingers tensing to dig in slightly. I wasn't showing yet, but I knew. Which meant I'd known what I had to do.

Was that why I hadn't killed Geoff? That was the original job, even if Sam hadn't thought I would actually *do* it. My handler had passed it off as a directive from Control, from the Agency itself, and he'd gone an interesting shade of pale when I told him it was a confirmed kill.

Didn't matter now, did it.

The kid sat up, staring at me as if I'd been rumbling in subvocal, too low for warmbody ears to hear. I came back to myself with a start, blinking. "What?"

"It smells good." He pointed at the spitted things, fat crackling as it dropped into the fire. "Are they . . . for eating?"

"Yeah." I remembered the house I'd taken him from, and the red smell of spaghetti sauce. "You can eat solid food, right?"

"Oh, yeah. It doesn't have to be . . . the other. Though that's good. I always felt hungry." He hugged his knees, and it wasn't my imagination. He was looking a lot healthier than he had. No longer as gaunt, and the essential difference in his face wouldn't be so noticeable if I could get enough calories into him. Calories, or . . . the other. I could calculate the calorie content in bodily fluids, but I didn't want to at the moment.

I nodded, as if it was the most normal thing in the world to be sitting here in the Waste talking about his liquid nutrition. "That house. Where I found you. They were your parents?"

He shrugged. "Dunno. I barely knew them."

Well, that's odd. "How long were you there?"

"Month or so, maybe. Before that, it was the institute." He hunched down, making himself even smaller. "They all had a design on their coats. Then one day, I woke up and there was a different design, and I was supposed to go to school."

Now *that* was interesting. His semi-neglected state made more sense now, and my brain chewed lightly at the implications.

Thermascan told me the meat was safe enough now, nothing bacterial or parasitical likely to be wriggling in it. "You know how to eat these?" For a subject change, it was a good one.

"No." Hunching even further, those big dark eyes holes into a frightened animal.

"Neither do I." I got the spits situated, and dug in the gear for eating utensils that might possibly work. "We'll learn together."

That seemed to ease him. At least, he scuttled forward to help, and he was the one who figured out how to crack the bones and suck nutrient-rich marrow out. His teeth were strong and sharp, no sign of the baby fangs he'd displayed while . . . drinking.

"Abbymom?" Tentatively, licking his greasy fingers to clean them.

"Hm?" The calories were welcome, even if I could live off solar. No need to make the nanos work any harder than necessary. The little guys want to survive, and they do a damn good job of keeping an agent together, and some agents are pretty cavalier, using "almost-invulnerable" as an excuse for being careless.

Not me. The easier I make it for the nanos, the more efficiently they keep me functioning at peak. I suspected I'd need every erg of their help sooner rather than later.

Geoff forged onward, stealing little glances at me. "You're cyborg, right? But you're not one of *them*."

"Who's *them*?"

"The . . . corporation. The scientists. Doctors, bodyguards. *Them*." A shadow of a snarl, much too old for his young face. "The ones in charge."

I don't blame you for feeling that way, kid. I took a deep breath. "I'm implemented pretty thoroughly, what they call a flexible liquidator. I worked for the Agency—those big black mirror-boxes you see all over the City." I paused. "Now I don't."

"Why not?"

The firelight leapt and danced, painting shadows on the cave walls. All the tech that had created both of us, monuments of human engineering, and we ended up sitting here in the rocks, eating scorched meat from over a fire.

"Because I didn't want to liquidate you." *What the hell's that?* My scans were picking up disturbing activity. Not thopters, that was good; but like every good thing, it had a sting hidden in its ass. I cocked my head, sorting out the impressions, and was hard put not to sigh. "Now listen to me very carefully, Geoff. This might be unpleasant."

I let them think they'd caught me sleeping, and they knocked me on the skull to make sure. Fortunately my reinforced brain-case is more than adequate to most occasions.

The hardest part was feigning limp unconsciousness. Big men and small, a few women too, all in tattered odds and ends bleached by the harsh conditions. The females reeked twice as badly as the males, probably a survival tactic. They joked about how heavy I was, and cuffed Geoff once or twice, but he didn't resist and they simply tied his hands together and set him on one of the pack beasts, with my body slung over in front of him. He kept patting at me, his hands a soft sweating metronome, as we rode through darkness and chill.

The desert had grown cold. Sandy soil creaked and shuddered underfoot, far-off rumblings moving through as the swarm of predators bore their prizes away. The fourpads were hooted over, the gear pawed through. One or two of the men fiddled with my trousers but decided not to go further since the nanos were pumping out pheromone mist through my skin to wilt any carnal urges. I could have just shut off with a trace subroutine running to wake me when it was over, but the thought of the kid seeing that was just . . .

Well, I didn't want to. He'd seen enough.

If any among them were halfway intelligent, they would have thought the absence of celebratory rape a little odd. Fortunately, they were scavengers and bottom feeders, and one of the hallmarks of Adison's ketosis is the fogging of higher cognitive functions.

They probably thought they caught us completely unaware, despite stinking to high heaven, all filthy with sweat and other crustings—dirt, dried blood, eliminations, rotting vegetable matter. I could have shut off my nose, but I needed all the information I could get. Unfortunately, they spoke in a weird gibberish, only faintly related to Spanics and loaded with too much grunting and slang for me to get more than a rudimentary sense of what was being said. Not that it mattered much, all I needed was that unmistakable breath of sickly-sweet ketosis-cloying on them to know that one thing about the Waste was true.

There were cannibals after all.

They tossed my body into the same cage as Geoff with a few sickening chuckles and a final hurrah, while firelight painted the night. It was a camp the size of a village, tucked in a network of caves about eight and a half klicks from where they found us. Grease-ruddy glow painted soot-smeared edges, and there was a throbbing of drums that could give you a headache. The barred door slammed shut—wooden, probably pretty sturdy if you weren't implemented, and secured with a length of rusty flexcable most likely scavenged from a long-ago thopter crash—and our captors melted back into the main area of the caves to join the whooping and drumming.

I sat up.

Geoff, crouching next to me, almost went over backwards. He was filthy—they'd rolled him in the sand a little.

It was child's play to get the bindings off my wrists and ankles, then I worked on the messy, knotted rope around his thin wrists. He was trembling, and when I got his arms free, I did something I'd never even thought about before.

I gathered him up, pulling him into my lap, and held him. The shaking eased bit by bit, and he whispered that name, the one I'd dredged out of memory and given him for whatever stupid reason, over and over again.

"Shhh," I said into his hair. "It's okay. It's all right. I told you, didn't I? They have a use for us."

"Abbymom . . . Abbymom . . ." He moaned a little, a trapped, despairing sound.

Shit, this kid is going to be fucked up. If he survives. If we *survive.* I caught myself nuzzling him, breathing against the top of his head where oils and heat concentrated a child's scent-markers, and confusion swamped me for a second. What was I *doing*?

I'd never held a kid. I didn't even think I'd ever want to, and considering some of the more arcane aspects of implementation, it's pretty impossible for me to spawn now. I could play if I needed to, but I was a dead end as far as the gene pool went, and it had seemed a small price to pay at the time. A baby in the Projekts was a stone weighing you down; runners had to be light.

I had been getting older, and slowing down. Also, skimming from shipments to pay for the dilate-and-cauterize had been a stupid but unavoidable move.

The gang of runners who'd caught me on that rainy night hadn't been out for turf or blood. Temporarily bonded into a group by alcohol and hebrox, they'd simply been looking for a little fun, and whichever one left me with a little growing anchor in my warmbody uterus probably didn't even remember that evening.

Later, the hole-in-the-wall hardcoin-only clinic, the "doctor" a reject from Ring medical practice, my feet in the cold stirrups and the bright white light in my eyes. At the end of the scraping and sealing, with the single shot of painkiller swiftly receding and the doc glancing through my already-fading mediflex chart again, salvation happened.

Look at those measurements. Right in the optimal range for implementation. Bet the black cubes would love to get their hands on you.

Just like that, a way out appeared, while I was chewing over and over what I was going to do when the druglord I was currently running for discovered my skimming. The cramps wore off completely an hour later and I scavenged homeless for a few days anywhere that wasn't near Cirquit or the Projekts, mostly the edges of the Ring suburbs where I could crack a trash sealer or two and get some food. Then I'd hied myself to the biggest, shiniest black cube downtown, a sleek sharkfin rising even above the skyscrapers of the major megacorps, and presented myself as a candidate for implementation testing.

The back-alley abortionist was right. They took me.

Yet another irony: eight and a half years ago, I'd scraped a new life out of me and signed myself over to the Agency. Probably just as fetal-fish Geoff was swimming in a vat, or sealed into a warmbody carrier's rented belly. Who knew how they'd created him?

I'm no kind of mother, dammit.

I didn't quite have the heart to tell the shivering bundle in my arms. Instead, I found myself rocking back and forth a little, while the whooping in the main cave-chamber echoed and crested, audible waves on a deadly shore.

The cannibals were celebrating. They'd probably seen the train wreck and picked it over pretty thoroughly during the hot afternoon, and no doubt Geoff and I had left tracks. Everything but a big blue-neon Cirquit sign pointing out the fact that there'd been survivors, and in their stupidity they probably hadn't thought too deeply about the casualties. Probably dragged themselves all over the scene and had a feast, if we were lucky.

I could have fought the ones who took us, and my first illogical thought had been to. Then tactical thinking took over—they would have a use for live survivors, because the fresher the meat the better, right? It served my purposes admirably. Their sloppiness would confuse our trail, possibly distract any pursuit, and now I had a much larger pool to draw gear and necessary information from.

All I had to do was wait. And hold my not-child, while my almost-invulnerable body performed an instinctive comforting movement older than civilization itself.

The drums didn't fade until near dawn. A few of them had stumbled back to hoot at us in the cage, but the reek of fermentation on them was so strong they probably didn't notice my hands were free. One pissed through the bars, laughing, and I smelled incipient kidney failure in the proteins leaking into the stream of urine. Added to the toothrot and the smoke, the fug of unwashed bodies and the distinctive odor of Adison's ketosis, you had a stench so thick you could cut it with a plasticine spork.

Geoff huddled against me, dozing, but he stiffened when I stirred. I'd moved a little before then, of course, cycling through the muscles to keep them ready.

Really truly freezing gives away the game, and one of the first things they teach you in agent training is how to pass for normal again. Always more efficient to pass; if the vast mass of sheep could pick us out of their ranks, they'd be wary. The Agency found out a long time ago that people do just fine with the merest semblance of propriety, rights, or freedom, polite fictions preferred over an uncomfortable truth. It's why people stay in the Cities, it's also why they say it's possible to pay off your implementation debt. Most agents don't really believe it, but the fact that someone cares enough to lie to save their feelings averts any real trouble.

The flexcable holding the door shut was rusted almost clear through, but it had some stretch left. I lifted the door slightly, slowly so the hinges didn't have a chance to creak, and motioned Geoff through. He moved almost as quietly as I did, and in the gloom his eyes reflected oddly.

"Can you see?" I whispered, and he nodded.

Interesting. I slid out bit by bit, my concentration narrowing to a single small point. There was a slight crackle as I had to distend my left hip joint a bit, but it only took three and a half minutes before I could gently, gently ease the door shut, the stress-sounds from the cable's stretching and releasing fading into a low hum of unhappy metal. I dropped down on all fours, shaking my head, strands of dark hair falling around my face as I breathed in, deeply, restoring function and letting the nanos work on the sore, stretched ligaments around my hip socket.

I could have just broken it, but I'd had a chance to plan, and this called for a little more subtlety.

Geoff crouched next to me. His eyes were huge, the pupils more oval than circular. How had they passed him off as human? Especially around the prized alphas and betas in corporate schooling? So much about the whole damn thing didn't add up. If my handler or the Agency wanted him extracted instead of liquidated, why hadn't they *told* me so? Instead of clumsily carrot-and-sticking me when my psych profile clearly stated I didn't work kid jobs? Nothing under eighteen, that was the one refusal I ever gave them. I'd performed every other job quietly, efficiently, and with a minimum of wasted resources.

Doesn't matter now, does it. I unfolded myself, tested arms and legs. Everything working fine, nearly tiptop. Geoff crowded close, and I ruffled the coarse silk of his hair before I could stop myself.

I bent down, put my mouth close to his ear. "I'm going to work," I whispered. "While I do, you need to stay where I put you and be quiet. I'll come back to get you, and then we'll leave. I know you're tired, but we have to move, and you've had some sleep. Do you have to . . . to eliminate?"

He shook his head, his cheek bumping mine. The thought of those tiny, pearly, very sharp little fangs sent a weird zing down my reinforced spine.

"Do you need to drink?" Meaningful emphasis on the last word, so he couldn't possibly miss my meaning.

Another shake of his head.

"Any questions?"

Three *nos*. I closed my eyes, running over the scans I'd taken when they carried me in, the layout of the cave complex and its inhabitants called up behind my eyelids as if I was preparing for a rooftop run, dodging statbolts and bullets, outthinking other runners who would just as soon drop you and collect payment for your cargo at the other end. Eyes that would turn you in, knives that would sink into your back—even inside an incorporated tribe of runners there's not a lot of loyalty. Only strength, and the instant yours fails, there's always someone ready to step over your still-warm corpse.

It was great training for Agency work. Or even just for living.

When I opened my eyes, I found Geoff peering at what he could see of my face, his teeth sunk into his lower lip. They weren't the distended fangs, but they still gleamed in the semi-darkness. The firelight wetly licking the crusted, weeping walls had sunk to an emberglow.

I moved slightly, and he closed his eyes while I planted a kiss on his forehead. That seemed to work, because when I straightened, his expression had turned far more relaxed. He wasn't shivering anymore, either.

"Okay," I whispered. "Let's go."

By about 3 am, according to my internal chrono, we were finally far enough away. I chewed on a bar of freeze-dried from the train's medikits—the idiots had dumped all their loot into a single pile, making it easy for me to take what I wanted. I'd burned through solar and was operating from internal energy, and that takes replenishing. The sand had turned to indigo, spangled and outlined with silver starshine and the light of a nail-paring moon. We were leaving the large rocks behind, but there were still smaller stone piles and caves, gullies and treacherous shoals at the edge of every pond of just-sand.

Just before Geoff and I had crept with our fourpads into the open air, the clamor had begun behind us, heavy toxic smoke filling up the lower caves—because the webbing I'd used to suspend nerve-blot canisters over the main fire had finally been eaten away by a judicious spray of cephannic acid easily extracted from a scavenged personal fuelcell. Add to that the leader of the monstrous hive—clearly marked by his habit of sleeping on a raised dais in front of the open fire, almost swallowed by a slumping pile of bones and tattered oddments—silently eviscerated, with plenty of his muscle mass as well as several bloodstained trinkets scattered around the bed of his grog-deadened third-in-command, and finish off with his second-in-command's two closest subordinates killed too, and what did you get? A fine internecine rivalry that would keep them busy murdering each other for quite a while.

Figuring out who's who isn't hard in that sort of tribal setting. You just look for who has what percentage of available resources, and rank them accordingly.

The chaos would muddy the waters of any pursuit, and our trail would be long cold if they even realized we were gone and not casualties of the melee, taken out of our cage and eaten in a corner.

It was a good bit of work, although not nearly the caliber of other turf wars I've started at the Agency's behest. Not bad for thinking on my feet.

Geoff rode in front of me, both of us squeezed into the saddle; the second and third fourpads followed placidly. They seemed much happier with traveling during the chilly dark, only nervous when a thundering under the sandy soil began. It wasn't a human commotion, but I didn't care to know what it was.

Not yet.

It was there—with a sleeping child in front of me and rivers of stars overhead, the east paling and dew coalescing out of thin air—I was able to turn all my resources to figuring out something that had bothered me all along.

. . . Woke up and the uniforms were different, and I was supposed to go to school.

NifulCorp was the badge on his school uniform. I'd assumed they were his creators, but perhaps that wasn't necessarily so. The two warmbodies in the house with him were security, not parental figures. I hadn't seen other monitors, but I'd been buffered and almost invisible to anything other than physical cams as a matter of course. A Ring suburb means *security* and you don't get that without eyes watching every angle, whether videoscan or otherwise.

The Agency could have been contracted to steal the kid back for his original creators, but with his very existence a revolution that could kick implementation right in the teeth, well.

The only flaw in this chain of logic was my handler's reaction when I said I'd killed the kid, just like he'd told me to do.

One thing was certain. I wasn't the first person who had stolen Geoff.

I was, however, determined to be the last. The next step was to find somewhere to shelter him from the inferno of daylight.

The thunder drew closer, our fourpads suddenly sidling and making wary little chuffing sounds. My knees clamped down to keep my restive beast going the right direction, icy sand crackled underfoot, and I sighed. My scans were picking up something very large.

Looked like something else was true about the Waste as well.

The worms.

CHAPTER THREE

TOWNSHIP VEGA

At first, I thought the township was a worm.

We found out worms are slower during the cold nights. They're big, and they move through the sand at will. They don't scan as animal, vegetable, *or* mineral, and there's a queer warping around them that could be anything from magnetic resonance to a stat-field precursor. They stay out in the open, where the sand is a sea. They don't often venture into the rock-stacks, so if you have to cross an open bay or inlet, after dark is always best.

By this time we were used to the dust, the weird vegetation, the scorch and the freeze. I could see in infrared, Geoff was like a cat in the dark, and moving kept us warm. During daylight we holed up in rock-stacks, the tough-as-old-transports fourpads cropping at whatever spiny succulent vegetation clung to the surfaces, surviving on dewfall and hidden veins of flat, horribly alkaline water. I could drink it to stave off fluid loss, but Geoff wasn't so lucky.

Fortunately, the plants were full of moisture. Geoff wasn't an herbivore, but that much food meant there were hordes of little prey animals around.

The only problem was catching enough of them. Between their cargo of meat and copper fluid, I managed three meals a day for him at least.

When we crested a short rise and I saw the lights in the distance, a strange pulse shivering through cold air and throbbing into the subsonic, I immediately reached for the stat-rifle slung in its case on the saddle. Halted midway as commchatter fuzzed into existence at the very edge of my sensing range, and tasted the air. No breeze, but now that I knew to look for it there was trace ionization cropping up clear as a statfield's signature.

"What is it?" Geoff whispered behind me, keeping below the sightline until I motioned him forward. He'd taken to riding on the fourpads pretty well, and even though his liquid nourishment was intermittent he looked . . . well, healthy. More like a kid and less like an alien.

Or maybe I was just getting used to him. "Supplies."

"What kind?" Always full of questions, but he stayed well back.

"Looks like a settlement. Pretty big, probably a full township, can't tell if it's corporate or not yet."

"Are you going to kill them too?"

"Only if I have to." It would have bothered me, but I was too busy planning, the glucose uptake around my well-cushioned brain in its reinforced case spiking nicely. "I can't kill *everyone* we meet, Geoff." *Just most of them.* "Come on up and take a look."

He did, his fourpad gnawing a cud of half-digested material. Their digestive systems are interesting, meant to strip every bit of moisture and nutrition from pretty much anything they can chew. Almost as good as the nanos, I guess, adapting to survive. Where do you think the cybiologists got the ideas for implementation from? A natural law.

They just wanted it sped up a bit, that's all.

We were down to the two fourpads we were riding. The other one had lasted a long time, but in the end, when it's a pack animal or your kid, you make the only choice you can and you hope.

"You really can't kill everyone we meet?" He sounded very dubious, and I almost winced.

"That was imprecise," I told him. "I can if I have to. It just isn't efficient. Now, we're going to ride into that township before the worms twelve klicks to our east get any ideas. I think that subaudible thumping the town's got going is a facsimile of a territorial call, to keep the worms away."

"Worms." He shivered, a flash of his teeth in the dark. Starlight played over his pale face, died in his inky hair. "You know they sing, right?"

Sure they do, kid. "Let's go."

I probably should have listened, but I was thinking instead about what I was going to do if it *was* a corporate town.

There was a statrepeller field, but it slid right over my skin with a tingle and I motioned Geoff through. He stepped through the shimmer and dust crackled away, the fourpads blowing out through their reopened nose-slits and sidling a little, dissatisfied. No security cordon, but the way the sand was disturbed just inside the field told me they patrolled fairly regularly. A group of twelve riding fourpads, not bad. Someone here was organized.

Geoff shook his head, twitching from the field. I forget, sometimes, what it was like to be unbuffered. "Tickles," he said, and my mouth made a small movement, almost like it wanted to smile. A huge physiological tell, shouting to anyone around the exact nature of my feelings.

Cut it out, agent. Take a look around. Be very careful.

The bleached, thin-skinned buildings had their backs to us, glossy solarcatch panels lambent as they discharged spare oxygen; condensation ran down microchannels and probably was fed into filters underground. Cheap, robust tech, but probably the biggest investment anyone could make around here. There were skinny, needle-eye alleys; the main avenue ran north-south, which told me this place had been planned and was on a travel axis.

The fourpads didn't like the sudden close quarters, but I got us squeezed through the largest of the alleys, every sense and channel open. By the time we stepped out onto the main thoroughfare, melting out of a convenient pool of moving shadow as the pulse of prem-torch light cycled down the street, I was pretty sure it wasn't corporation property.

For one thing, the saloon we'd been edging along the southern wall of was rollicking like a thopter in a magnetic storm, which is normal even in corporate towns, but the woman with her face to the netting over a coop of rustling bundles of sleeping feathers didn't have a monitor tag, and the man grunting as he stabbed her from behind with what he no doubt thought was his biggest weapon, to judge by the stream of obscenities he was pouring in her ear, wasn't augmented at all. The woman gave every audible appearance of enjoying herself, but her pheromone balance shouted *not aroused, thank you.*

I didn't think about what Geoff would make of that as we passed like ghosts—or at least, as much like ghosts as two shaggy beasts, an agent, and an eight-year-old genetically-engineered boy could be. I was too busy scanning the main thoroughfare.

Population: around 2,500, give or take. Lots of strangers, a lot of through-traffic. Garage at north end, saloon middle, slums south. Some agriculture evident, probably collectives who trade in barter, where is the tech—ah, junkyard there, that's where all the security is. Attached to a convoy station, there's an aquifer under here if that geo signature tells me anything. I pushed my fourpad's nose away from my hair—the damn beast seemed to enjoy cropping at it, maybe thinking it a plant—and glanced up at Geoff, who was craning to get a better look at the loving couple further back the alley. I clicked my tongue, softly, to get his attention, shook my head. *Don't stare, kid. People notice.*

He probably couldn't help it. Those huge dark eyes in that pale little face, in a town where everyone was likely to be burned dark, were giveaways. I'd have to see what their dry-goods depot would have in the way of bronze spray, and what I could trade for it.

I didn't think they took flex bitcoin out here, even untraceable, and I wasn't sure they'd take hard bitcoin either. That was City currency, and if this wasn't a corporate town, well, they might work solely on barter.

All that could wait. I guessed where the livery would be, took a deep breath, and put on my bargaining face. I hoped it wouldn't take too long.

I wanted a drink.

I hit the swinging doors just hard enough, and Geoff scurried in my wake. The saloon swallowed us with fauxsmoke and a healthy dose of another, harsher vapor I never thought I'd smell. Burning *nicotiana*, loaded with carcinogens and cut with something else nasal receptors identified as faintly soporific. The place served both ersatz and grain alcohol, and it looked like grain was the bigger seller.

Warmbodies are so fragile, you'd think they wouldn't go straight back to the killing chemicals once they got out of the corp-owned warrens. On the other hand, I'd always wondered about grain alcohol. It was supposed to taste better.

The music, clunked and wheezed out by a shipwrecked hulk in the corner that appeared to be some sort of instrument, tinkled to a stop as a bespectacled, scruffy-bearded gent craned his neck to see the new arrival. The bar was three deep, there was a wide space in the middle of the building crammed with warmbodies full of light, cheap augments doing something they might have called dancing, and most of the tables hosted men looking at greasy rectangles of paper stamped with corporate logos, circuit-chips in piles in front of them. Probably playing Betrisq, I thought, noting the number of cards in each hand and what I could see of the suit the man with his back to me was holding.

Geoff peered around my hip, clinging to me. I wished he wouldn't, any indication of weakness was not the best first impression. Not if you expected to avoid trouble later.

Still, the faces and voices were probably a shock after so long with just me to talk to, and whole nights spent with only six or seven words passed between us. When he wasn't asking every damn question that tiptoed through his odd little head.

In here, be quiet. I do the talking. Clear? I was hoping I only had to say it once.

"For Chrissake, Cameron, you ain't preachin' tonight, play the synth!" someone yelled, in passable Spanics.

The synth-player scratched under his mended suspenders and shook his head, light glinting off his oculars—wire-rimmed reworked Trefware, durable but with a disturbing habit of fusing onto the bones of the orbital socket. "*Dios*, forgive these sinners," he all-but-screamed at the rooftop. "They know not what they do!"

"Who slipped Cam the booze?" The bartender was a slight

woman with long dark hair and green-gem eyes, an expensive bit of implementation that probably wasn't coded in pre-birth. If it was a vanity augment, she'd come down in the world afterward, because the rest of her was in layered oddments that almost managed to disguise the sheer amount of weaponry she was packing. "And you, goddammit, if you make any trouble in here I'll cut your heart out. Keep playing, *Ortodoxo*."

The preaching synth-player rambled off in a stream of something that sounded a lot like New Orthodox chanting, but the synth—if that's what it was, the thing sounded like a spavined holo stuttering garbled skinspray adverts—began to tinkle away through a ditty I'd never heard before. The rest of the crowd began to hum along in varying pitches. Apparently it was a popular tune.

Great. I had to elbow a bit to get up to the bar, Geoff clinging to my side like a runner's satchel. You have to wear them high and tight if you expect to skate rooftops, but with his nose at bellybutton height for me he was too big to haul in a sling and too small to elbow on his own account.

The bartender watched this with a great deal of interest, her hands almost blurring as she mixed and dispensed. Her throat swelled a little—subvocal implant, probably an accountant and dictation tab. The arrangement of weapons handy behind the bar, camouflaged or not, was thought-provoking. She was well prepared for any drunken trouble.

An agent, though . . . not so much.

She was also handling the money without a looksee over her shoulder. *Ah. Not just the bartender, then.* "Evening." I pitched my voice just loud enough to cut through the noise.

"Ain't you polite," she yelled, husky and amused. "What you want?"

"You Laurel?"

"That's Madam B to you, damn your City ass," came the pert whipcrack of a reply. At the other end of the bar two men, both caked with dust and rancid grease, erupted into a shoving match. She paid it little mind. "Coy sent you?"

I had no idea who Coy was. "Nope. Livery said you had rooms."

"Livery's got a damn sense of humor." She sized me up again, and Geoff peeked over the top edge of the bar. I dropped my weight and threw a hip, and the man crowding in to see if he could get a handful of breast on my left stumbled back, losing his place at the bar. "You got hard bit?"

Cautious relief warred with nebulous unease inside me. "I do."

"And what else?"

Nothing you'll subtract from me. I gave her a sunny, feral smile. "A deep desire for peace and quiet."

"Ha. Show me." She slapped a shiny key fob down on the bar, I slapped down a round bit of circuit-etched hard currency, and she grinned at me, revealing implemented teeth filed to sharp points under those bright-green eyes. The teeth were only half as pointed as the intelligence moving around inside that warmbody skull, and if not for her metrics—I was cataloguing everyone around me out of habit—she would have had a shot at implementation. She was probably Waste bred and born, though, if her mane was any indication. It had none of the sleek lifelessness of hair that's never seen real sunshine. The Wastebred weren't allowed into Cities. The risk of a stray bit of mutation left over from the Wars laying waste to a City's screened genetic pool was just too high.

That's also why Egress trains are sealed. One of the *official* reasons, that is.

We exchanged the little bits of metal at the same instant, and

I didn't twitch when she spun the bitcoin and made it disappear. Which made her pupils dilate unsteadily for a moment, and that interest in her gaze sharpened, bright as a runner's payday. "That your kid?" Her chin jerked down, indicating Geoff, who balanced on the brass rail some of the men rested one foot or another on.

My right hand ruffled Geoff's hair without any conscious direction on my part. "Yes."

"Don't look a thing like you." She studied him, studied me, and opened her mouth to ask another stupid question. My face changed slightly, my left cheek twitching by a single millimeter's worth, and maybe she decided discretion was the better part of valor, because she thought better of it. "The girls will love him. *Hey, Skye!*"

A tangle of arms and legs on the dance floor birthed a tall, lightly implemented woman, her breasts threatening to break free and run amok from the strips of leather she wore in place of a shirt and her long legs lost in a fluff of pastel skirts that showed bits of unbronzed skin. She moved with a knifefighter's supple grace, and the blades on her were plasilca—they carried a stat charge if you handled them right, were wicked sharp, and held that edge better than metal. Their habit of flexing during a fight meant you needed implemented reflexes to even begin to handle them right. The hair-thin scars she'd covered up with bronzer on her arms showed where she'd tried to swing them around as a warmbody. She was lucky she hadn't opened an artery doing that, and when I scanned a little closer I found out her implements might be light, but they were quality work and her reflexes were probably at half-agent speed.

Even more interesting.

"This is Skyedawn," the owner-bartender shouted, over the noise. "She likes kids. Room Eight, Skye. Be nice."

The woman rolled her eyes, her hands busily arranging the froth of skirts she wore—once-vibrant spincotton faded from repeated chemwashing and probably hung to air in the volcano of daylight. She cocked a hip and beckoned as another man stumbled for the bar, his mouth wide open and working under the brim of a hat studded with circuit wire and bits of bone probably from the little furry creatures we'd been living on as we traveled.

"*MADAM B!*" he roared. "I GOT CREDITS!"

"Oh, *damn* it all," was the owner's reply as she waved me away.

We followed the tall woman up the stairs, and that was how we arrived in Township Vega.

Geoff curled on his side in the bed, knees drawn up and face slack with exhaustion. The place had chem and waterwash, a luxury I wanted to spend at least a half hour in but I settled for just a quick sluicing. Running our clothes through the ancient stat-cabinet got most of the crusted dust off; neither of us sweated like ordinary warmbodies. One more thing to be grateful for.

I tucked my damp hair behind my ears, smoothed the ancient, threadbare blankets over him. Below, the throbbing of crowd noise and tinkling of the synth merged into a heartbeat. The room was small, the wooden furnishings patched-together and handmade instead of metal and mass-produced. If not for that, the shuttered window, and the smell of fresh desert air working its way into every corner, it might have been a womb-like little warren in the Projekts, the pulsewaves of flying ammo and the crackle of adverts on loop providing the background instead.

I let out a long breath. Straightened, scanned him from top to toe. The longer we were out of the City, the more his scans changed. You could have mistaken him for a human kid before, if you just glanced, but now the shadows of the internal organs were . . . different.

He seemed okay, though. He blinked, slowly, those big dark eyes distant and the scar on his chin pale instead of flushed.

He'd need feeding soon.

"You thirsty?" I touched his hair again, smoothing the dark, rough silk. I'd trimmed it as well as I could a few days ago, with a pair of scissors found in the cannibals' loot pile, and he looked far less unkempt.

He shook his head, his cheek soft against the rough linen pillowcase. "Not yet. Are we going to stay here?"

"Just for a little while." I touched his temple. A non-implemented skull, so fragile. Thin bone, with no reinforcement. "We're going to have to keep moving."

"For how long?"

As long as we survive. "For a while. Don't worry about that right now."

"Okay." He closed his eyes, snuggling into the pillow. "Abby-mom?" A whisper, barely audible under the music downstairs.

"Hm?" I couldn't stop stroking his hair. Each strand moved differently, a fascinating interplay of light on the keratin sheaths. He seemed to enjoy the touch.

His eyes, half-lidded, gleamed. "Will you kiss me goodnight?"

I hesitated. "Did they used to do that? At the institute?"

"I saw it on holos." His own hesitation, a shadow of hurt on that transparent face. He pressed against the bleached linen pillowcase. "You don't have to."

I bent and pressed my lips to his cheek. It was plumper now, not so gaunt. The Waste agreed with him, I guess. "Goodnight, sweetheart." The word felt odd. Not because I shouldn't have said it, but because I'd never done so before. "I'll be downstairs for a bit." *If I ever needed a drink, it's now.* The alcohol wouldn't do anything, but the slight flush from metabolizing it sounded wonderfully soothing.

"Okay. 'Night."

I passed my fingertips on the scanpad for the rickety metal tensor lamp standing on the small, indifferently painted nightstand. It dimmed, and when I pressed the second pad near the door the room became yet another dim cave. His breathing was already evening out and deepening.

I closed the door before I could say something even more absurd and headed downstairs.

The next day passed slowly, Geoff so deeply asleep he was barely breathing. I cycled through rest and REM, stretched out on the thin carpet. Even though they had statfields over every door and window, the sand still worked its way in. My hair would get full of grit, but that didn't matter much.

The nanos can get rid of toxins, renew cells, and keep the body going virtually indefinitely. It's the mind that needs sleep—the skullmeat itself or whatever consciousness nestles inside it, they haven't been able to figure out. Even the nanos keeping fatigue poisons out of the brain didn't halt the need.

The vulnerability of surcease is balanced by alarms and subroutines built in through both implementation and hypnotraining. The hypno's for when you're a warmbody, to prep you for the transition. For some reason, agents don't respond to hypno once implementation's started. Your first dose of nanos cures you of subliminals.

Which is good. Who knows what mental Dismiss switches they'd put in you otherwise? Besides, over-susceptibility would rob any agent of the required flexibility and moderately rebellious streak. You can't think on your own or do creative problem-solving if you don't have both.

There's a lot of below-conscious thinking that goes on when you're cycling. Most of the time, it's where you do . . . well, not all the planning, but all the stuff that makes the planning *possible*, and a lot more effective.

Breathless-hot dusk settled over the township, the sun sinking. It was nice to not be hiding in a pile of rocks, and really nice to be able to get my full complement of cycles in without jerking into wakefulness every few hours as an animal scratched inside my scanrange. The noises of people around me were just comforting enough to lull, not a wrong breath, nothing out of place.

We're social creatures. Even agents. What woke me was Geoff's slight stirring, his padding into the bathroom to stand in the chemshower. When he was done, it was time to get some calories in him.

The downstairs, empty at this hour, looked a little forlorn. Nevertheless, the tables were ruthlessly scrubbed, the worn-glossy floor swept and polished, and smells of cooking bubbled through the entire edifice. Wooden shutters clasped the large cornglass windows, and the bars of westering sunlight poking through were enough to give the whole picture a surreal golden glow full of floating dust.

Grain alcohol is just as useless to me as ersatz, though the nanos like the carbs and give me a pleasant all-over flush metabolizing the poison. Agriculture out here depended on watermakers scavenged or leased from City corporations, but the end result was real bread, some of it from maize-mash. Plenty of fermentation byproducts in the starches to add vitamin value. Protein that wasn't vat-grown—which meant there was some kind of system for raising and slaughtering livestock, good news for Geoff since we'd figured out his liquid nutrition didn't necessarily have to be human. There was very little in the way of vegetables, but lots of fruit harvested from the spiny plants fourpads liked so much. Their sweet, semisolid insides packed a great deal of nutriment in a small space.

All the warmbodies and heartbeats around me in this building were female—dancing girls who earned on the side in the usual way, the owner, the three women who scrubbed floors, mopped, and collected laundry. The ones that were implemented had light, high-quality work, and they were a disparate bunch. After a little observation, I decided Madam B had probably helped finance no few of them, and her little saloon was turning a tidy profit that kept being reinvested.

She was, by far, the most humane corporation I'd ever seen.

The man who had been torturing the synth last night shuffled in, yawning, just before full dark rose. Evening heat simmered off him as he shrugged out of a few long, loose layers, revealing a New Orthodox cassock underneath, its top unbuttoned a little to show a threadbare spincotton shirt and those much-mended red suspenders. One of the dancing girls brought him a bowl of stew, and he brightened considerably. He reeked of metabolized alcohol, staggering to a table not far from the shadowed corner I'd picked.

Skyedawn brought a tall, crooked plasilca glass flu of a pale, slopping fluid, setting it near Geoff's bowl of corn mash and fruit. "Drink."

A quick scan showed an emulsion, proteins and sugars and acids. Geoff peered at it, his nose wrinkling. "What's in it?"

She stared at him for a long moment before flicking a quick judgmental glance my way. "Milk."

"I've heard of that. It's like calc tabs." I relaxed slightly. "It's safe, Geoff."

He reached for the glass, tested it, and his expression went through several odd little shifts before settling on cautious approval.

"What do you say?" I prompted.

"Thank you," he mumbled, looking back down at his bowl.

The tall woman's judgment visibly shifted a few degrees. "He your kid?"

What do you care? "Yes." There was a block of salt on the table; you shaved off bits carefully with an eating implement or a weapon. I'd read about a time, far before the Wars, when it was used as currency, but out here they probably had vaults full of the stuff.

"Don't look nothing like you." She made a quick movement, and I almost twitched. She probably didn't guess how close she came to choking on her own blood, she just crouched, folding her arms on the table to put herself at Geoff's level. "Cute. What's your name, *chiquito*?"

He glanced at me, I nodded fractionally. "Geoff."

"I'm Skyedawn."

"I know." He took another drink. "This is Abbymom. She rescued me."

"Rescued you, huh?"

That's enough. "I'm sure the nice lady has work to do." Calm and polite, but a warning nonetheless. Geoff looked back down into his bowl, but he didn't turn pale or flinch.

Progress. I might have felt just a little absurdly proud.

"I'm off." Skyedawn's teeth were implemented, reinforced for durability and in some cases replaced. Looked like the same work the owner had. Maybe there was a dentist in town, too. Who knew the Waste would have good implementers wandering around, as well as the necessary tech? "Just making conversation. You come from City, don't you."

Is it that obvious? Of course it was.

I set my spoon down very carefully, heavy potmetal scrubbed free of tarnish and reasonably germ-free. "Convoy route passes through here. Lots of City people." I didn't try to mimic her accented Spanics, but when we next hit civilization anyone who heard me would swear I was from this little burg.

"Oh, sure. But convoy stays at the depot. Not many waltz right into Livery between arrivals."

Just fishing, or more? No hint of anything in her autonomics, her pulse normal, her respiration even. Not even a stray dilation of her pupils to show a lie, nothing off in the chemicals tainting her sweat. I contented myself with a noncommittal noise.

She waited, but I didn't react. When she unfolded herself, drawing up to her considerable height, it occurred to me that her bosom held no implementation. It was a natural wonder, so to speak.

Lucky girl.

"I'll bring you some more *nophala*, Geoff," she announced. "And if your Abbymom isn't nice to you, all you have to do is tell us."

Geoff gave her a long solemn look. His free hand crept across the table and touched mine, our fingers interlacing, and I didn't move as she swung away, maybe satisfied, maybe not.

Instead, I watched the stat-veiled door, every inch of me pulled tight against itself as if I was in the City again. There was something familiar in scanrange.

A subroutine clamped over my autonomics, squeezing my pulse back down, copper adrenaline laid against my palate before the nanos started soaking it up, leaving just enough to prime me for action. I squeezed Geoff's hand very gently, then freed my fingers, squashing the urge to reach for the rifle in my lap.

It wouldn't do any good.

The door swung back and forth, its statrepeller field fluorescing—warmbodies wouldn't see it, but when a buffered body moves through, the lumens spike-cycle predictably, and an agent watches that range as a matter of course.

Tall, wheat-haired, his eyes piercing gray. For some reason nanos won't touch iris pigments, even though lots of other things are pretty plastic if you can get enough fuel for alterations. He stepped in, brushing fussily at his sleeves, in worn-down bleached-out clothing that managed to look halfway local, just like mine.

I was already on my feet, the rifle left carefully on the bench.

I could mark "ramming a lectric shivprobe through his chest and popping his Dismissal switches" as the last time I saw the new arrival, or "dumping pieces of his stripped and trussed-up body in a vat of caustic sludge." Choices, choices.

It was Sam, in the flesh, just walking in the front door as if this was a normal meet, him giving me the Agency's marching orders. Winding me up and setting me in motion.

And if my Agency handler had shown up *here*, who else could be not-so-far behind?

CHAPTER FOUR

SAM

He marched right up to the long cobbled-together bar, a loose limber stride just a touch too long to be natural. It kept him out of strike range, and the peculiar grumble of subaudible—standard for meets—thrummed through my audio intakes.

"Hullo, Jess."

It would be ridiculous of me to stand near the table. Besides, the further he was away from Geoff, the better. Nothing else in scanrange, everything as it should be. Had they cordoned off the entire township?

If they did, I'm going to have to get creative. "Sam." My own subaudible grumble, none of the warmbodies around us would pick up anything amiss. I stalked to the bar as well, just out of physical range. If he was walking in like this, he obviously wanted to talk. Or to delay me.

Which meant I had time. Not a lot, but some.

A small grimace went over his bland face, just a fleeting expression. Other than that, he was flatline as usual. Just the messenger, passing the news along. My own autonomics were the same. He was handler, I was flex liquidator, and I'd already killed him once.

Time would tell if I could do it again, now he knew I was capable of attempting it.

"Whiskey, please." In audible range, sunny and polite, he may have even winked at the owner. I could have told him charm wouldn't work.

Madam B eyed him for a long moment, and he sighed theatrically, fingers flicking and a flash of hard bitcoin sparkling on the bar. It magically produced a drink; she gave me a long considering look, glanced at him again.

My lips curved in a facsimile of a smile. "One for me, too."

"Sure." She poured, a long amber stream of liquid, and I took the shot, cracked the bottom of the glass against the bar with just the right amount of force. Her eyes narrowed as she sized both of us up. "No trouble inside, folks. It's the standing rule."

"He's just here to talk." I gave Sam a sidelong glance, stayed audible. "Isn't that right, Sammy?"

"Never knew why you called me that." Another fractional grimace. Maybe he was looking for an emotion-of-the-year award.

Then we're even. "Jess" as a name is strange, even from you.

"It's alliterative." I considered the glass. Heavy, and cornglass fractured if you did it *just* right. The edge was good, but it would be the thick base that was most helpful, if I twisted it around his eye and savaged one-half of his optics. "Mild. Fungible. Short."

"Thanks." He switched to subaudible again. *"You're looking well."*

Empty compliment. My heartrate and respiration nice and even. *"Mad at me?"*

"Let's call it pleasantly surprised. That the kid?"

Subroutines, clamping *hard* over everything. I smiled, gazing at the flyspotted sheet of cornglass mirror at the back of the bar, every warmbody and item in the room marked and alternatives clicking over inside my head. *"Told you, target eliminated. As far as the Agency's concerned, he's dead. You keep it that way, or it won't just be a nice bath you get."*

I probably shouldn't have gone straight for a threat. It was a psychological tell the size of a blackbox Agency building, but at this point, he had to suspect I had an agenda where the kid was concerned. I just didn't want him to know precisely what *kind* of agenda.

Not yet. Not until that bit of information would serve my purposes.

Again, he switched to audible. "You've created problems."

I'll just bet I have. I've been trained for it, after all. "What kind?"

He studied the mirror too, probably making some of the same calculations I was. "I can help you. If you let me."

I've heard that one before. "Not interested, thanks."

Our gazes didn't meet. I knew I was faster, implemented for liquidation. A facilitator, however, might be smarter.

Might. And there was no way he could get as brutal as I was prepared to.

Sam sighed. *"You're in over your head, Jess. If you want to stay alive, you'll give me the kid and we'll both walk away."*

I pushed the glass along the scarred top of the bar, slowly. Sam produced another hard bit; Madame B poured him another shot. He took it down, exhaled softly.

There were so many things I could have said. *Ever study biology? Did they ever teach you anything about bears? Extinct now, but ferocious as fuck, they had claws and teeth, and when you came for their cubs, they got mad.*

That was too close to a clue. I could have threatened him again. I could have informed him that he'd take the kid over my dead body, and if he wanted *that* he was woefully understaffed, no matter what he'd brought with him.

All of it was empty. If he had Agency backup it was just a matter of time.

Do things efficiently. Save your strength.

I settled for looking at his face. Studying the line of the jaw, the pulse of his well-reinforced carotid, noting his metrics again. He wasn't as optimal as I was for implementation, but he was close. What was he doing walking in as if he owned the place? I wasn't that big of an Agency asset, there was no need to handle me with kid gloves. Did they have a pulse, lectric or otherwise, prepped? It wouldn't do any permanent good, I was buffered.

So was he. The most they could do was incapacitate me for a short while.

Audible, again. "Jess. Please. I don't want to see you Dismissed."

Awful concerned, aren't you. "You make it sound like it would be easy."

He paused. Then, the crowning absurdity. "Whoever you're working for, we'll triple it, and bring you in safely."

This made the second time I laughed out loud in a bar talking to my handler. It was getting to be a habit. "Now I *know* this isn't Agency business. Who owns you, Sammy?"

"You wouldn't believe me if I told you."

"Likewise, I'm sure."

"Come on, Jess. Running out of time."

Aren't we all. I turned, giving him my back, but only an idiot would have jumped me then. He didn't, and I aimed for the shadowed booth.

The New Orthodox synth-torturing priest was observing this with a great deal of bleary but bright-eyed interest, spooning his mush in. He was right in the strike zone, and if Sam jumped me now there was no way the priest would ever play another tinkling little jig on the ancient instrument again.

The moment passed. Geoff looked up at me, and that haunted, frightened expression was back, plastered all over his face with blue Cirquit neon. My throat had dried, for some reason, a new thing to subroutine. Did the kid think I was going to just hand him over? I bent slightly, braced for any impact, and spoke as softly as I could while still remaining warmbody-audible. "Things are about to get a little noisy."

"He's like you," Geoff whispered, pale little words. "Is he here to kill us?"

I'm fairly sure he wants you alive. Which is not as reassuring as it could be. "When it starts, you go upstairs," I said. "Barricade the door. Don't open it for anyone but me." I searched for something else to say. *I'm probably going to get killed* wasn't reassuring either, was it?

Neither was *I'm sorry I wasn't smart enough.*

"When's it going to start?" A flicker of his tongue, nervously wetting his lips.

I didn't blame him. "Pretty soon." Because my scans were picking up activity now. Very subtle, very quiet, but definitely activity.

Which could only mean one thing. *Agents*. Multiple. It was time for me to get creative.

The first place I was going to start was with my handler. But he was already moving, ghosting out through the swinging door. Which was odd.

Really odd.

"It's started," I told Geoff. "Run."

Egress meant I couldn't take much in the way of agent kit with me. Plus, best to be safe and not carry anything even *remotely* traceable, right? Go light and fast, pick up gear along the way, a runner's habits. Always something lying around that'll help; people are trash-creating machines, and what's trash is often usable.

All of which meant I was facing multiple hostile agents with a TekStan hybrid statrifle, two projectile guns with variable-ammo capacity, a few interesting bits looted from the cannibals, and my own winged feet, as runners say.

I slid out through the swinging doors, skin darkening rapidly to draw in as much solar as possible from the dying sun. I couldn't afford another evisceration, not with multiple hostiles and my free source of energy about to take its nightly bath.

You do realize you're about to die, right?

No matter how thoroughly implemented you are, going into any fight makes the stupid warmbody part of you nervous.

Especially when you know it's a *losing* battle.

There wasn't a cordon—no thrumming of baffled thopters, no queer deadness of a commwall. Just four blips in my head, moving through a mental map of the township, too quick to be warmbody and too silent to be anything other than liquidators.

A short running start, a leap, and the weightlessness of almost-flying. A *whoosh* of air pressure changing as I landed across the street, a sun-bleached canvas awning giving resiliently underfoot, but I didn't apply enough force to tear it, only enough to *stretch and throw me;* another leap put me on the roof of the livery. At this angle I could see most of the township—and they, no doubt, could see me.

The comm channels were alive, six encrypted streams. So they were working together, and there were decoys or hidden agents. Sending four of them could mean they wanted to neutralize me and pick up the kid.

Or it could mean I was Dismissed.

Time to hope Barlowe really did get all my implanted switches out. The rifle socked into my shoulder, and a hot blue-white static bolt whined as it smacked a leaping paper cutout of a shadow. The shadow folded up like a spider flicked into a statre-peller, and even buffered that probably stung, because I'd caught whoever it was going fast.

There was a reason that out of all the hardware the cannibals or train robbers had been carrying, I chose this particular version of TekStan rifle. There was a batch of them dumped offmarket years ago, because nobody in-City would use them. They weren't high-powered enough anymore. Well, you *could* mod them, but they turned unstable when you did, and the oscillations could give buffers a hard time.

You just had to be crazy enough to go ahead and mod them. I was hoping the damn thing wouldn't blow up when I pulled the trigger any number of times tonight.

Another crunch, this one metallic. One coming in from the left, I fired off another bolt and flung myself back, my boots *scritch-scratch* on hardened tar sealant, and by the time another one streaked in to hit me from behind the township folk were starting to realize something was going on.

Of course, it could have been the shattering sound as I kicked one of the liquidators right through a propped-up solar panel. Sparks flew, static fizzing as I followed it with a shot from the rifle, twisting in midair and dropping as a repeater probe-bolt whizzed overhead.

Oh, no you don't. Another twist, aiming off the edge of the roof and bringing the rifle up, its recharge-whine almost at the right pitch. Next would come temporarily sacrificing the high ground to draw in whoever was hanging back and watching, because *that* would be the most dangerous of the bunch, the agent with enough brains to let everyone else throw themselves on the pile first.

Move. Weightless again, feet thudding on sand-grimed concrete, pitching forward to roll as a whisper of displaced air behind me meant someone had their wits about them. A stunning blow across my back, rolling again, up on my feet with my bootheels squealing and grinding. It was a male, taller and heavier than me, but that can mean next to nothing when you've got control of the situation.

I didn't. There was a high piping scream, punching through the noise of breaking glass as I socked my hip into the male agent's side and threw him into an ancient window of cracked plasilca strengthened with alloy bars. Geoff tore out through the saloon's swinging doors as I straightened. A last flash of sunlight threw all the shadows into high relief, the township's lights flickering into life and confusing the optics even more.

"*Abbymom!*" Geoff yelled, and the doors burst open behind him again.

Female agent, blonde and blue, in dark spinwool jumpsuit just like the others; her optics must have been upgraded with something, because they were full of a weird silvery shine, stuttering in and out as she blinked. She had to be the smartest cookie of the bunch, because she hadn't taken the bait and come for me.

Instead, she was streaking straight for my kid, and there was no way I was going to reach him in time.

Nightmare-slow, implemented muscles popping and even my nanos probably screaming as I bolted for him. *Too late too late too late*, and next would come the crack as she snapped his neck, or the explosion of burned meat and boiling blood, or maybe she'd just bury a blade or two in him. She could just grab and bolt, and then I'd have to not only fight off the other agents full of City gear and probably updated especially for this run, but also go after her and hope to hell I could catch her before—

Light. Searing, bright-white, I went down hard as the male hit me from behind again. Reflex tucked and rolled me once more, slapping the palm-held statpop switch against his neck. More crackling to add to the chaos; if he had implanted Dismiss switches they would be fusing—the statpop was Barlowe's little toy, one of the many I'd scanned thoroughly until I knew I could replicate them, a little bit of planning and forethought paying dividends yet again.

Quit thinking about Barlowe. He was a necessary casualty. There and gone in split-seconds, one of those stray thoughts that happen during a fight when you're hit bad and the body doesn't know it yet. Legs up, wrapped around the male agent as if we were Projekt kids playing acuesta pig-a-back, my fingers cramping slightly as his body bucked against the feedback. A *wrench*, hair tearing, the angle was wrong, we were still tumbling along the ground and he'd slowed me down too much. Another pull, my arm at an awkward angle, and cervical structures fracturing in a song of high stress.

More statbolts whined. *What the hell?* I shoved the male's limp body away, fish-jumping until I could get my feet under me, and was upright again just as a smoking body thudded down where I'd been lying a few seconds ago.

Oh shit, shit shit shit—

"*DOWN!*" Sam bellowed, and I dropped, landing on the smoking almost-corpse. Agents are theoretically invulnerable, but you can hurt us plenty, if you know how.

Another tearing sound, and it wasn't just a static bolt, it was a full-fledged ball of plasma, searing the air and raising every hair on me as it blinked through space. It hit another agent—male again, a real bruiser, probably did black-box or bodyguard work—square in the chest, and I would have winced if I hadn't had other problems. The commchannels were still encrypted, but stuttering wildly, random distress signals. This guy had the new oculars too, a flat silver shine over his entire eyeballs.

Don't they want to pass as warmbody? Who's fucking firing that? Did they miss? Am I just that lucky?

There was a heap in the middle of the road, in dungarees, those stat-taped boots, and a Static Rebe T-shirt torn by a scramble in some rocks the first time we'd outrun an early-waking worm. He was on hands and knees, shaking his head, dark hair shivering with reflected light and blisters rising on one cheek where the last flash of unfiltered sun had struck him. So small, and I skidded on my knees, smoke bursting from the tough reinforced pads on my dungarees as I grabbed him, folding over him as the plasma cannon roared again. The next shot would strip the flesh from my reinforced bones and might kill every nano in me; I squeezed my eyes shut, there in the middle of the road, and thought about how I was going to throw Geoff clear even as three-quarters of me was vaporized.

A smoking, humming silence. Footsteps. My breath coming in high hard gasps, getting enough oxygen in to fuel another desperate move, I tensed. No way to outrun a plascannon, the fucking thing was still live, I could *smell* the ionization. The kid trembling in my arms. *I told you to run,* I wanted to say. *Dammit, I told you to go upstairs and lock the door.*

Maybe he even *had*, and she'd gone in through the window. Now wasn't the time for debrief, and it wasn't like it mattered.

Any second now. Any second. A great stillness inside me.

"Jess," Sam said, quietly, "let's get these bodies taken care of."

My head turned. I blinked through the fog of combat and lifting smoke. Roasting, just like a cannibal feast—their nanos were going to have a hell of a time patching them together. If there were any of the silver motes that hadn't been knocked clean out of them. If even one remained, you could be fixed.

But it would be very painful.

Sam lowered the plascannon's sleek silver bulk from his shoulder. It began powering down with a sweet piercing harmonic that sent shivers all through me, and through most of the township's buildings as well. There were probably warm-body casualties. Hell of a mess.

I stared at my handler. He was scuffed up too, blood painting the left half of his face. Head wounds, messy, and he probably didn't get his hands dirty often. Facilitators, you know. Pulling strings, sitting behind desks, running errands, and passing along messages.

It was just like a number of in-City jobs, a facilitator pulling a liquidator out of the fire. Like the CranCorp core-handler fiasco, or the war between RebeBron and KalaskilGen. All those times he'd stepped in, because the facilitator is not only handler, support, and liaison, they're also the one who gets docked if they lose an agent outright.

"What the fuck?" I whispered, through dry lips.

A loose easy shrug, the plascannon's deep dark eye losing its winking pupil. It shut off completely, and the silence was immense. "I told you, I'm here to help."

If you meet a facilitator, you figure out pretty quick they're damn smart. What you don't see until it's crisis time, though, is that they can also talk warmbodies into just about anything. A combination of verbal facility and an acute grasp of psychology, as well as pheromonal control, plus something tests can't pin down. It's a sort of charisma, a dominance factor as well as an indefinable, just like a liquidator's psychological and moral flexibility.

Fortunately, he didn't have to display it in front of the kid. One of the benefits of agent speed is that you're gone before the dust settles. By the time the warmbodies had stopped cowering and started peering into the dusk, Geoff was trembling against me in a one-room shack at the end of the slums. The wooden walls—creaking as the desert turned from hot to cold and breathed all over Vega Township—were flimsy, but they kept us from being seen by warmbodies, and some of the other leaning, sand-eaten structures around us were even unoccupied.

Sam disappeared briefly and returned with our gear and fourpads, as well as a couple shaggy beasts of his own. There was fodder enough for them in the secondary shack leaning against the first, and the creatures settled into happily munching. I, on the other hand, was nervous as a runner approaching her first rooftop—something about those agents bothered me, but hard as I tried, I couldn't figure out *what*.

I was too busy keeping my ears perked for trouble, or Sam returning. Whichever came first.

When my handler slipped back in through the piecewood door, shaking dust out of his wheat-gold hair, I had the TekStan to my shoulder and Geoff behind me.

Sam sighed, heavily, and dropped the bar—just a heavy creosote-soaked piece of lumber—into the alloy brackets. It wouldn't do any good, since the walls were thin enough to walk through, but maybe it made him feel better.

"There's no need for that," he said, in plain audible. "I'm *on your side*."

"Pardon my teensy little bit of disbelief." The whine of a fully-charged rifle grated on my nerves. Geoff's ragged breathing didn't, but between the two sounds, I was having too much trouble keeping my subroutines tight over my autonomics. "What the *fuck*, Sammy?"

"Aren't you even going to say thank you?"

"Start talking." My hand tensed, ready to squeeze the trigger fully and sting him. That would give me enough time to wrench *his* head off as well, and this time I wouldn't just drop all his parts into sludge to keep him down for a little while.

This time, I was considering a permanent solution, and take his plasma cannon. I could use something like that. It was the entire reason we were still where he'd left us with a muttered *stay here, for fucksake.*

"I was going to get the kid out of town." Sam lifted his hands, slowly, and rubbed at his face. After years of seeing him betray no emotion at all, it was a little shocking. His hair was beginning to take on the roughness of out-City fur. "Someone wants him set free."

"Free?" A laugh boiled right under my breastbone, but my control was better than his. It didn't even get close to the surface. "That's a joke. You gave me a kill order."

Geoff didn't twitch behind me. He pressed close, his face against the curve of my lumbar spine, as if he could blot all this out just by making everything dark.

Sam dropped his hands. They looked different, too—a little harder, growing calluses the way a Facilitator never did. "Your psych profile said you wouldn't kill a kid, Jess. More importantly, *I* didn't think you would, either."

"Oh, I will if I have to." My autonomics started to realign, settling under the subroutines instead of fighting them. "Just not this one."

That earned me a long, appraising look. He folded his arms, blond-tipped eyebrows drawing together a little, and it occurred to me that his signaling emotion could be a trap. Or it could be genuine. Either way, he was a liability, even if he had just saved both of us.

Why would a facilitator after a rogue liquidator do what he'd done? Plasma cannon can blow all the nanos out of you, and if you don't have even one left in your meat you're on the fast-track to oblivion. It's possible to save an agent that's been hit by a plas-blast, but it requires quick action and a stasis tank, and I didn't think they had filtration and stat-neutral narcofluid, let alone gallons and gallons of restraint gel, out here in the Waste.

I might have expected another liquidator to use plas against me, but not a facilitator.

Maybe whatever lie he would tell would still give me something useful. So I gave him some bait. "Niful stole him from someone else. The Agency was contracted to steal him back, but decided he represents a kick right where it hurts—in their bottom line. And you. Who the fuck are *you* playing for?"

"You wouldn't believe me if I told you." He tilted his head a little before settling into fully implemented immobility. "Is he okay?"

"Like you care." I didn't ease off the trigger. "Answers, Sam. Now." I'd never held him at gunpoint before.

There was a certain charm to it.

"Niful stole him from someone else, yeah. The Agency wanted him for study and dissection. We wanted him out of the city." Slight emphasis on the *we*, as if he didn't think I'd catch the implication and wanted to give me a clue. "I thought that after eight years of working with me, you'd come back and tell me there was a problem. That you'd ask me for help, and I'd get you both out—"

How very noble of you. Had he just thought I wasn't bright enough to figure out something in the damn job stank? "Why?"

"Like I said, you're my favorite. And your psych file was pretty clear you're just not the child-killing type, Jess. I suppose we should all be grateful for that."

"That's insulting. You're a crappy negotiator."

Geoff shivered, his breath hot through my shirt, a circle of damp on my back. The calculations were instant, instinctive, and hateful.

I could say it. *Take the kid.* Or just leave Geoff here with Sam suitably disabled for a short while. I could vanish into the Waste, and forget all of this. There would be no reason to pursue me after I made the cut.

In other words, true, absolute freedom. If I was just going at this from a personal survival standpoint, that was my best bet. Any other avenue, even with a possible fourth player—original corporation, NifulCorp, Agency, and whoever Sam was hinting at—muddying and jostling around, just ended up with a short suicidal run before someone dropped me and did whatever they wanted with the kid anyway.

Just put your head down and get out of here. Walk away.

I wondered what it felt like when the plas hit and blew all your nanos out. Did it hurt?

Another faint twitch of expression crossed Sam's bland, open face. It looked for all the world like disgruntlement. "I was *hoping* you'd have developed some trust in me. A rapport. Your file said you would."

Maybe the file doesn't know everything. And maybe I would have developed a "rapport" if he hadn't sent me to murder a child, even if he didn't think I'd do it. "You're another cog in the machine, Sam. Just like me."

"More like a spanner in the works; always has been part of your considerable charm." A ghost of a smile. "The offer stands. We'll pay you triple, whatever they've promised you, and we'll make sure you're safe."

That *we* again. A bluff, most likely. "Disap—" I squeezed the trigger midsyllable, and the flash was enough to blind even buffered optics. "—pointing, Sam." I'd deliberately kept my eyes open, not giving him even a blink's worth of warning. I shook my head, waiting for my optics to clear, rifle still held ready even though Geoff's trembling took on an intensity I didn't like at all.

Sam lay splayed on the floor, twitching. The modded rifle hadn't blown me up yet, and that was fantastic. Luckier than I had any right to be. He would be out for only a few minutes, unless I moved fast.

I shook free of Geoff and braced myself. Another high-harmonic squeal, and I found my breath was coming much harsher than I liked as I wrenched my handler's head from his body, tossing it across the room as the rest of him twitched and jerked. *Probably really uncomfortable. I'd say I'm sorry, but I'm not.*

With that taken care of, I turned on my heel. Two strides got me back to Geoff, and I went down on one knee with a jolt, grabbing his shoulders and examining him.

He stared at me, glaze-eyed and shaking. It made me wish I could just transfuse some of my nanos into him. If they wouldn't corrode him from the inside out, being tuned to my helix down to the last strand of RNA, I would have. I couldn't implement him, but shit if I didn't want to.

He was so *breakable.*

"Geoff." Quiet and firm. "It's okay. It's over. We're leaving now."

His chin trembled a little, the thick, seamed scar quivering. "Abbymom?"

"Right here, kid. I'm not going to let anyone hurt you." I winced even as I said it. Strict honesty would add *if I can help it,* but he didn't need to hear that. He had enough to deal with already.

I was no kind of mother, but even *I* could tell as much.

"You could have let him take me." Hearing his lost, forlorn little voice say it out loud was squirm-worthy.

I swallowed, hard, for no particular reason at all. There was nothing wrong with my esophagus. My autonomics were all running along smoothly. "I wouldn't do that, Geoff."

"Why?"

Did he really need to hear it again? "Because you're my kid."

"But you . . ." He blinked, sense returning to that dark gaze. "But *why*, Abby?"

I don't know. Only I did, I just couldn't explain it, and we needed to get the hell out of here. I needed to think about things, especially those agents with their weird silver eye-sheen, and I thought best while moving. "It's *Mom*, Geoff. *Mother* if you're feeling formal. You can top off with one of his fourpads while I go through his gear. I want to be far away from here by dawn."

CHAPTER FIVE

NIGHT MOVES

Stars, those faraway nuclear fires you never see through a city's statveiling, glittered on velvet blackness. Our tiny noises, fourpad paws shushing along sandy rock and the creak of saddles, were lost in the breathing of the wind. The Waste was a vast creature, and us just tiny motes caught in its passages.

Geoff didn't ask where we were going. It was just as well. I might have answered *somewhere nobody can find us*, and he was probably smart enough to know that wasn't a real answer.

At least we had a plasma cannon now, and some other useful bits of kit. Either facilitators traveled light, or Sam hadn't brought a lot of Agency hardware with him. Which was thought-provoking, if I'd had the urge to think about even more than was already crowding my brain inside its lovely almost-invulnerable case. Those silver-eyed agents—where had I heard something about them? It had to have been during my runner days, anything afterward I would have retained. One of the dubious benefits of implementation is a steel trap of memory. Very little escapes, once we have time to track it down.

We stopped late; dawn was almost up before I found a

suitable cave. Geoff picketed the fourpads, talking to them in a low whistle with tongue-clicks, maybe his own version of subaudible. The beasts liked him, tolerated me, and outright balked at going near worms.

Which was fine, I didn't want to get too close to the massive gray blind-snouted things either. The long segmented beasts didn't even follow the veins of water under the sand—in fact, they seemed to actively avoid anything that could be interpreted as moisture. It was a puzzle.

"Mom?" Geoff, holding the canteens. "They're almost empty."

"I'll set up the maker." I crouched next to the fire, feeding it small wisps of drought-stricken grasslike stems. The fourpads produced pellets that could be burned, though using them to cook seemed incredibly unsanitary even if I could thermascan the edibles for doneness.

At least Sam's gear included a sturdy little watermaker. I wouldn't have to worry about Geoff dying of dehydration.

Just hunger, maybe. Or that deeper thirst.

Geoff straightened. "I can do it." A little anxiously.

I nodded. It would be good for him to be familiar with that basic tech. "Go ahead, then." *Just don't break it.* I decided that would be an unhelpful thing to say. Stared at the tiny flames, willing them to live.

He dug in the packs, his dark hair wildly mussed and standing in stiff, soft spikes. It wasn't just my imagination—the Waste definitely agreed with him. Was he taller? It certainly looked like it.

How had *that* happened? I frowned, feeding another small handful of dried grass into the flames. I didn't know the growth rates for kids his age, I'd never had the desire to look them up. When would he reach maturity? When he did, would he be a little more durable?

It wasn't likely to happen soon enough to do me any good, really.

Come on. Do something productive, agent. "Geoff? What do you remember, about the institute?"

He settled down, his back to the pile of packs and gear set against the side of the rough stone hollow, opening up the watermaker's curved plascine case. Frowned a little at the components inside. "What do I do first?"

"Take out the base and tap the red button. That'll start the statfield to clear any dust away."

"Oh yeah. Okay." His frown deepened a little. "The institute. My room had toys. It was a big round room—a globe, sort of. Plasilca, so they could observe. Lots of doctors. None of them were like me, or like you."

"Like me? Implemented?"

"Yeah. They were all regular." He fitted the shine-black cylinder into the base, remembering to hold them a little ways apart for a few seconds so the statfield could repel any foreign bits. "They fed me cloned, ah, blood. Sometimes it had other stuff in it. Caffa, synthsucrose, alliums. Skin tests too, for infrared, UV, caustics, all sorts of stuff. Kept asking me about my dreams, what I remembered."

"What you remembered?"

"From Before." He peered at the top of the watermaker, setting the tubes correctly without any help.

"Before the institute?"

"Yeah. I never remembered much, though. Bright light. Being hungry. Lots of noise."

Did he remember being born? Or decanted, or whatever? Or . . . "You said they tested you for UV."

He shook his hair away, an irritable, very young motion. "Yeah. It didn't do anything. Nothing did."

"The UV didn't hurt you?" Well, there went *that* theory. So it was something else in unfiltered sunlight that raised the vesicles and the weals on his skin.

"Nope." A small smile, when he fitted the plunge and the gasket right on the maker.

I focused on the fire. All those different chemical reactions, spewing out heat and light and ash. He was a good witness, all I had to do was ask the right questions. "So . . . at the institute, they must have had badges. A logo. Do you remember that?"

"Oh yeah. It was an eye, with stuff shooting out of it. White and black."

That narrowed the field, but not as much as I liked. Most likely CoreTech. But they're strictly weapons and information, they don't do genengineering. Or at least, I didn't think they did. "Huh." I made the sound open-ended, neutral.

"I didn't have parents, like kids on the holos did. I wondered about that, until I figured out it meant they'd made me, like they made other things. I would watch and try to figure out . . ." He bit his lip, concentrating on aligning the top correctly. "When I woke up and the badges were different and I had to go to school, I thought maybe they'd found my parents."

It was enough to make me wish I had a cushy in-Ring job, enough to pay for a highly trained therapist. He'd need one. It might even be best for the kid to go back to his original owners—at least they'd given him toys.

They didn't protect him well enough. I might not be able to, either.

The fire solidified, just enough fuel to keep the reaction going.

I could tell you the composition of the rocks we crouched in, where water was hidden underneath, I could test the atmosphere, live off solar, kill the deadliest things in the Cities—other agents—without qualm.

What I couldn't do, though, was pretty much anything that might give Geoff a chance of, well, turning out a reasonably well-adjusted adult. If there was such a thing in the world we'd been given.

I really didn't think this through. Wondering if I was worse than the corporations fighting over him—if Sam really had been banking on me not being able to kill a kid and looking to get Geoff out of the City—was uncomfortable, to say the least.

He should've told me as much, dammit. "I'm sorry," I said, quietly, to the fire.

"Why? Now I have a mom." He grinned, shaking his hair back. It was such an open, unguarded expression something inside me cracked a little. "You even kiss me goodnight. It's good."

Except I'm probably going to die, and maybe you with me. Or they'll snap you up and keep experimenting on you. "I just, you know. Worry. About . . ." Pulled myself up short. There was no reason to add to the things *he'd* worry about, too.

"Yeah, I know. I think I put this together right." He examined the watermaker critically. "Wanna check?"

"I'm sure it's fine. I can set it out in an hour or so to charge." Not to mention sit beside it, my skin darkening, and gulp at all the solar I could get. I added more chips to the fire. Maybe it was a waste, I didn't need the heat. Did he? "Are you hungry?"

A shake of that shaggy head. "Not thirsty either. I just wanna sleep."

It was enough to make me long for warmbody unconsciousness as well. "Go ahead. We should be okay here."

Flickering shadows turned his face into an older boy's, for a bare second. You could almost see what he'd look like in adulthood—long nose, thin mouth, heavy eyebrows. "Why do they still want me?"

Not sure. "Could be a lot of reasons. So far we have three other players in the game."

"Game?"

"There's the original corporation—sounds like CoreTech—and then there's NifulCorp. Then there's the Agency. They survive by having a lock on implementation. You're a direct challenge to that monopoly."

"What about *him*?"

It took me a second to follow the mental leap. "Oh, Sam? Not sure which one of them he's playing for."

"And what about you?"

Yeah, kid. What about me? So I used the oldest trick in the book—when you need a moment to think, feign puzzlement or temporary non-auditory intake. "What?"

"You were Agency, right?"

"Was, yeah." *Not anymore. I doubt they'd have me back. I'm a losing investment. Unreliable.*

"And then?"

"Then I wasn't anymore."

"Why?"

I'm a bit hazy on that myself. I stared at the fire some more, as if there was an answer hidden in the space between fuel and reaction. I never told another soul, from my corpclone parents to my fellow runners or other Agency trainees, about the clinic or the bundle of cells scraped out of me, probably sold to bring a little more profit in for the medical staff.

It didn't belong to the Agency. It was mine, it was *private*, and I kept it that way, even when they asked, over and over again, why I wanted to be implemented. Why I was *volunteering*.

The Agency was, quite simply, a way out. And now that the kid was asking a similar question, it made me squirm a little inside, thinking that maybe I'd looked at him and seen a way out, too. I was a good flex liquidator, fast on my feet and efficient, but sooner or later even Agency jobs got . . .

Boring. When you're practically indestructible, you end up just going through the motions. Nothing matters. It's all the same.

Geoff needed an answer, and he was waiting on one. I took a deep breath. No reason to tell him I didn't fucking know why I'd done it, but once I'd lowered the rifle in the bare, security-locked NifulCorp house he'd been stashed in, it was too late. I was in, and when you're in, the only way through is to put your head down, your betrisq chips on the table, and finish the game.

I heard my own sigh, and couldn't tell what was going to fall out of my mouth until it happened. "Because you need me."

He carried the watermaker, stepping gingerly on sandgrit rock. Settled beside me, close enough for his warmth to meet mine. After a few seconds, he leaned into me as well, his small shoulder against my upper arm.

"I'm glad you found me," he said, quietly.

"Me too." I surprised myself again.

Because I actually meant it, and I slid my arm around him. It felt natural to tighten it just a little, to give him a gentle hug.

It did not, however, stop the way my brain inside its knock-proof container kept running lightly over all the players in the game, because I couldn't figure out which side—or *sides*—Sam was kicking the ball for.

I'd left his head and his body in a room together. It was only a matter of time. Why?

Because even though I could have brought his head with me, I suspected he was eventually more helpful to Geoff alive, no matter *which* side he was on. I was hoping I was right.

* * *

Dusk fell in great purple and orange veils, finding us already moving with Geoff well-wrapped against the sinking sun. The water table was rising, which meant the worms came closer to the surface as a matter of course, and the big gray blunt-snouted monstrosities seemed to be hungry.

It made little sense, really—what did they live on? The tiny burrowing things in the sand? If they did, or if they lived on the sand itself, why did they rise and snap at anything crossing the surface?

Maybe they were just cranky.

The fourpads plodded along. As the water table rose, so did more of the succulent greenery. Which meant more mammalian life. Catching them for Geoff to drain was getting easier. At least we hadn't had to sacrifice a fourpad yet.

Small mercies.

While I rode, I tinkered with a stat-coil and two or three Pankorip circuits. Plascannon knocked the nanos right out of even a buffered agent, there wasn't a way to reroute that sort of flux. Something about the resonances temporarily made your own flesh repel the tiny things that made near-immortality possible. The less implemented you were, the more you stood a chance of surviving plas—for a few seconds, at least, before slipping into shock from the roasting, your bodily systems shutting down one by one.

Quick death or horrified numb descent into blackness. Which was worse?

No way to buffer it. Hard to dodge plascannon balls, they tend to seek out their targets. Moving just made a disturbance that pulled them along, freezing let them home in on you as well. Discharging a cannon inside a City was a good way to make *every* corporation that held a share of the place get a vested interest in Dismissing you, because the Agency played hardball with anyone taking their ventures out *that* way.

None of the corporations wanted to piss the Agency off. At least, not that openly.

It was a puzzle. The best tech minds couldn't solve it, and me cobbling spare bits together wasn't going to uncover anything new. Still, it was something to keep my hands occupied. Maybe I was deconstructing under the stress of aimless running.

I hoped not.

A crackle at the edge of scanrange jerked my head up. It wasn't a worm.

Huh.

"Mom?" Geoff, his fourpad crowding mine, was unwrapping his hands. Neither of the beasts were uneasy yet, and the sun was just below the horizon.

"You hear that?" I swallowed the other thing I wanted to say—*don't take those off yet, it's not really night.* It was close enough, and coddling him that way would be counterproductive.

He cocked his dark head. His eyes reflected the dusk differently than a warmbody's, and those stiff spikes of hair bounced a little since he'd taken his hood off too. "Not really. I just . . . feel something. It itches."

"Itches?"

"Yeah. Like it did before you showed up. I knew something was going to happen."

"Where precisely does it itch?" Now there was a question I never thought I'd ask anyone, ever.

"All over." He shifted in his saddle, a little all-over motion expressing mild discomfort.

Well, at least it's not localized itching. I don't know if antibiotics will work on you. "Huh." The crackling in my scans resolved into fuzzy static, rising and falling.

Commchatter. None of it with encryption-spikes. The bands were sloppy, too, not tightly disciplined. A blurring buzz throbbed at the lowest end of my audible intakes.

What the hell is that?

A few moments later, I had the answer.

"Skimmers." I checked the sky—the last fading dregs of sunlight swirling down the western drain. The rocks were too far behind us for hiding. The sound jagged in and out of the edges of my range, not quite randomly. "A hunting party."

"Are they after us?" Anxiously crowding his fourpad even closer, as if that would solve the problem if they were.

"Don't think so. Probably cannibals, though."

He winced and I might have laughed, only it wasn't very nice laughter. It wasn't helpful, either. He needed me calm and steady.

Geoff glanced fearfully around, though the skimmers were nowhere near. "Are we . . . are they . . ."

I decided to answer the most obvious questions instead of whatever he didn't know how to ask. "No. This time, if they come for us, I'll fight."

He pushed the goggles up on his forehead, blinking furiously. "What do I do?"

"Stay out of the way." *That's all you can do right now, kid.*

"Why didn't you fight before?"

"It wasn't efficient."

"Oh." He relaxed a little bit. "I thought . . . you weren't afraid of them?"

Not very. I searched for a way to explain it. Agent training had only covered it briefly, because of complete autonomic control. Runners have several different theories about the whole thing, none of them quite satisfactory. In the end, I just decided to give him my personal view. "Fear's a natural response, Geoff. It'll keep you alive, make you sharper. Until it doesn't."

"And then?"

"Then, you put it away."

"How do you do that?" Brightly interested, his head up and his nostrils flaring as he sniffed the wind the way he'd seen me do it. "Ions. And something else?"

I nodded. My fourpad swayed, working up a slight rise, its large feet spreading against the sand. "Fuelcore dumpoff, the wind's right to start smelling it now. If there was one way to put the fear away, kiddo, someone would make a mint off selling it."

"I smell something else."

I took a deep lungful, in snuffles to pass maximum air over every sensing cell, organic or otherwise. Most of taste is smell, and even warmbodies get more information than they can possibly process in every breath.

They just don't pay attention.

"And?" I prompted.

"Green." He nodded, then snuffled just like I had. A pleased smile showed the white tips of his teeth, and I realized with a jolt that he *was* taller, by a good inch, than he had been in-City. "I think it's going to rain."

"Huh." I tried the air again.

No hint of petrichor. Just the same dry wind, nutmeg tang of baked sand, scorched rock, fuelcore dumpoff, ions . . .

The thrumming resolved into five engine noises. Definitely skimmers, and their comchatter was full of slanging Spanics, crackles, and obscenities that would burn your ears off if you let them.

"Mom?"

"Hm?" I closed my eyes as the fourpad picked its way along, pointed down the opposite side of the dune it had just climbed. It might be nice to have a skimmer, but Geoff couldn't drink from one of those machines in a pinch. Locking their commchannels gave me a better handle on location, especially since skimmers are loud in every sense of the word.

"How do you shut off being afraid?"

"That's the secret," I told him. "You don't. You just make up your mind to *do*, no matter how scared you are."

"Oh."

"It's harder than it sounds, and you have to do it a different way each time. Looks like they're not going to come near us, they're chasing something else."

A slight sound—his hair shifting. He'd tilted his head even further, probably aiming his dominant ear to try and catch something, anything out of his warmbody range. He stiffened in the saddle. "I know what they're chasing."

"Do you." I didn't even try to sound convinced.

"A worm. Only they don't know something."

"What don't they know?"

"They don't know that it can see them."

Active imagination, or something else? "Those worms don't have eyes."

"He doesn't need them."

"Why not?"

"Because I've told him where they are and what they're doing."

My eyelids flew open. Geoff's were closed, and he swayed on the back of his fourpad with loose, uncanny grace. Dark falls swiftly out in the desert; one by one, the stars were glimmering into life. It was a good thing moonlight didn't give Geoff any problems; whatever it was in unfiltered sunlight didn't bounce off the big white rock in the sky.

Or if it does, it doesn't make it through the atmosphere. Huh. I flagged that line of thought and set it away for a little bit. Maybe there was a solution there. "How have you told him?"

"They sing. *Inside*. You just sing back." As if it was obvious, like breathing or walking.

"Okay." I didn't bother arguing. I just kept building my map of their hunting pattern. Five jackasses on skimmers weren't a huge danger in and of themselves, but the chance that one of them would paste my fragile warmbody kid with a stray lucky shot was unacceptably high.

The skimmers veered again, just at the edge of my range. The commchatter was alive with excitement, rough words and male bonding. When they get together in packs, they urge each other on. If you want someone who hunts alone, make sure they have ovaries.

Boys always like to show off for each other too much.

We plodded on for a while. Geoff half-asleep in the saddle. He hummed, a low wandering melody I didn't recognize, but I was busy keeping tabs on the skimmers. They looped a little closer, slid away.

I had almost relaxed when the comms dissolved into a welter of feedback squeals. It almost jarred me out of my own saddle. I yanked on the reins, bringing my fourpad to a halt. Its shaggy head lifted, ears flicking as they rotated to catch whatever its silly two-legged rider wanted next.

The noise lasted ten minutes, all told. One comm crackled with desperate sobbing breaths before a final squeal of tortured metal ending on a crunching snap.

Then, silence.

Geoff's humming dwindled. His fourpad stood obediently next to mine. After a full sixty seconds, his eyes opened sleepily. He blinked. "Are we stopping?"

My throat seemed dry, though it wasn't. Purely psychological. "Not yet." I coughed, slightly. Another tell. It would have given Sam a pause, probably unsure if I was displaying to provoke or mislead—or honestly reacting to an uncomfortable thought. "Can I ask you something, Geoff?"

"Sure." Heartbeat, respiration, all going along normally. Warmbodies didn't have that kind of control over the autonomics. You needed implementation for that.

Or did you?

"What else do you hear singing?"

"Some things." A yawn half-swallowed the last word. You wouldn't think he'd spent all day sleeping. "Big dogs. They sort of croon. The worms are all squeal-y. There's small things, they get sleepy when it's too hot or too cold, but sometimes you can hear them going *sssss*." A hiss between his teeth. "You don't have a song, but sometimes people do."

"I don't have a song?"

"Not one I can hear." Did he sound suspicious? Frightened? Or just tired?

He was only a kid. *My* kid.

"Hm." I gathered my reins. "The water's rising even more. We should see actual green in a while."

"That'd be nice. It's going to rain, Abbymom."

"Sure." *You know, Geoff, I think I'm starting to believe you.*

Stripped to the waist in the glare of sunlight, my skin burnished ebony to suck in all the solar it could, I had plenty of time for thinking. No fourpads for this, they were in a small outcropping of rocks several klicks south. With Geoff sleeping so deeply he almost didn't seem to be breathing, it was safe enough. Still, better to do this quickly.

So I ran.

I've spent most of my life running, one way or another. Mostly along rooftops, gauging routes and ducking when I had to, outthinking, always a few steps ahead. It was often so laughably *easy*. The world is a ki-fait board, but everyone's playing chong-qi, that ridiculous little child's game that always ends the same way. When it wasn't easy it was stupid, and when it wasn't either it was boring to fight it. Much better to just retreat and let them boil in their own vat of genetrash.

Running shook everything loose. Loping along, not fast and not slow, a comfortable pace at about three-quarters. You never showed your speed if you could help it. Or your strength.

Or anything else.

Of course, implementation means not-fast-not-slow is still a blur to warmbodies. The sun showered me with free energy, powering tireless muscles and reinforced bone, flushing my nanos with strength. On the sand, leaping at random, rolling sometimes—going down, shoulder to back and the world turning over, up in a shower of dry particles worn into powder by the wind and the same sun that filled me with crackling force.

You were always my favorite, Jess.

I never asked why he gave me that name. He never asked why I called him Sam. Meets in restaurants, alleys, occasionally in seamless, perfumed corporate highrises. Always the same. Never a blip, just passing the message along, telling me what the Agency wanted from me since the first brief meeting at headquarters—the very same black cube I'd presented myself at for testing.

Six years ago, when I was still new to an agent's speed and strength. Fresh off the implementation line and upgraded to the max, sold into slavery by my own hand. They didn't call it slavery nowadays, but I knew what it was.

It's impossible not to.

Hullo, Sam had said, his bleached-gray irises piercing but not overly striking. He looked just like every other corpclone, his costume carefully chosen and his every move correct. Not polished enough to be slick, not rough enough to be green.

Right in the middle. *Looks like we'll be working together. Here's a list of drops. Commit it too memory and then get creative with destroying it.*

My own instant almost-dislike, squelched ruthlessly. *Creativity is not my problem, sir.*

A long, considering look. *Call me something else, will you?*

Yes, sir.

Not even a grimace. If I'd irritated him, it didn't show. He turned, a military little movement, then he was gone. I scanned the paper. Easy drops, none of them difficult. Maybe he was watching to see what I'd do, or maybe the Agency was.

So I popped the paper into my mouth, chewed, and swallowed, and that was that.

My stride lengthened. There was a trembling underground I didn't like. Tuning my ears to echolocation meant I'd have to filter out all sorts of other input.

What I really wanted to do was think.

So, I ran.

They sing, you know.

You even kiss me goodnight.

Bright light. It was cold.

What had they made? Or . . . Made, or *found*? What if . . .

He's my kid. I'm the last person to steal him, dammit. Mine.

A corporation getting hold of him again might even be good for him, until he didn't earn out. Wasn't that what he said, looking at a cyborg pointing a rifle directly at him—a cyborg who had just killed his two caretakers? Or his protectors, his jailers—whatever they were.

I'm an investment. I guess I'm not earning out.

I slowed, slightly. I *really* didn't like those rumbles under the sand. Acid in a digestive system would be uncomfortable, but I was fairly confident of my ability to burst free of even the massive worms east of here. I could be the last meal one of them would ever eat.

That will slow you down. Be efficient, agent.

The only thing is, there's something you can never escape. It matches you pace for pace, it breathes with you, it moves with you. There's no outrunning it.

Yourself.

I crested a long, shallow rise, kicking up great gouts of sand. The rumbling under my feet sent tiny flakes of it up and down, small rocks from below popping free of the surface like water spattered across a hot impulsion coil.

Wreckage scattered across a depression in the sand. The hole was shallow, shaped by displacement. Four or five skimmers, flung in twisted bits, scarred with acid or something caustic. The sand was glazed—I rolled and came up again, the back of my hand numb where it touched the creeping opalescent trail. Some form of analgesic, maybe—psychoactive compounds in it, the nanos perking up to analyze and neutralize.

Isn't that a useful little chemical mixup. Nice molecular chain. Wouldja look at those peptides.

The long, shimmering trail looped for miles. The worm had burst up through the sand, wrecking the group of skimmers. Not only that, but it had chased its pursuers, now on foot. Maybe the skimmers had irritated it, so it struck at the metal contraptions first?

Or maybe it had someone singing a little song about what to do with the insects buzzing overhead. What do you think, agent?

I leapt atop one of the piles of wreckage. Settled instantly into an agent's immobility, the eerie stillness you learn not to use when you're around warmbodies. Out here, it just made you a rock.

Would it be so bad, to turn into one? No struggle, no striving, no protecting fragile, breakable things—

It broke over the rise, the great gray snout rising from rivulets of sand greased with that opalescent sheen. A blunt, eyeless head, its mouth with circular rows of serrated, backward-pointing, milky teeth.

The smell was familiar. I inhaled sharply, no need for chuffing to distinguish one thread of scent-molecules from another. Not with the thing so reeking-close and streaking closer.

It humped along the surface with oily, terrifying speed and drew itself up, foot after foot of ringed gray flesh. The sun striped it with steam—was the UV damaging it? Or was it just moisture loss from the oven of daylight, hammering us both flat in this cup full of shattered metal?

Only rags of the bodies left. Probably ate them. Might eat the skimmers too, look at those teeth.

Closer. Closer yet. Roaring. It exhaled all over me, and I saw those teeth actually *moving.* Revolving, ready to grind anything it could into a pulp.

That mouth looked downright painful. And it could take me in one gulp. Still, when you are very small and facing something very large, maneuverability counts. I had already calculated its trajectory.

Noise like an Egress Train crashing as it roared, the sound fuzzing across several different bandwidths. A jolt. I went flying, already tucking and rolling, skidding on the slimy residue still not dried by the heat. Tumbling, sand spuming, and the thing went over me, its bulk more sensed than seen, more felt than heard. Like taking a drop off a roof, *knowing* the wave of flying projectiles from the rival druglord's cannon mounts was a breath behind you, you'd done everything you could and the next few moments you just relaxed and fell. You'd done all your planning, judged all your distances, and now it was time to see if you were really that good, or if you deserved to be splattered.

Adrenaline against my tongue, bright copper. Sand and more of that goop showered down on me, small rocks, crystalline bits, tiny glittering things.

It could have swallowed me, I suppose. It was fast enough. But instead, the worm went right over, and dove deep. The thunder of its passage faded, leaving me standing in the middle of a skimmer junkyard, rolled in slimy sand, and breathlessly laughing at the sheer impossibility of the whole thing.

I reached the rocks after noon, checked the fourpads—happily chewing on those succulents, now growing larger and larger the more southwest we tended. More plant life probably meant more refugees and castoffs from the Cities—or more Cities themselves, squatting like toads on resource veins—

I froze.

There was the sleeping-roll, the light blanket. The packs he liked to rest his back against. The scent of my dusty little boy all over the material, and watermaker, put together perfectly, set right by my own spot across the ring of stones containing ashes of the morning's fire.

"Geoff?" Even as I said it, I knew he wasn't eliminating in the back of the cave, or curled in a dark corner.

He was, quite simply, gone.

CHAPTER SIX

HE'S TAKEN

Carsona was a corporation town. It was also close enough that the skimmers could have been raiders picking through its refuse, or even inhabitants out for a joyride. Geoff and I would have avoided the place, but whoever had taken him would have come through here.

Or at least, so I hoped. Whoever it was, they hadn't left a trace. Not even a thread of scent. Had Geoff surfaced from sleep and gone outside to find me? Unlikely in the daylight, but it could have happened. I hadn't even left him a note—not that we had any paper, anyway.

I shouldn't have left him.

To top it all off, he'd been right. It started raining.

The clouds raced in like greased cargo containers down a magchute, and a wall of water crashed down on the desert. Rivers poured off slanted solarcatch panels, gullies opened up in the sand, the three streets—because Carsona was bigger than Vega by a long shot—became quagmires, and the entire township staggered under the weight. The late afternoon was a steam-hell, the sun doing its best to reassert its primacy but unable to reach through a pall of heavy, blackening skyveil. Thunder rolled, and it was my first time hearing sky-collisions without a City's muffling dome of stat-veiling.

It was also my first time feeling raindrops untainted by City smog or condenser-wash. The reflexive chemtesting in my skin returned some interesting results I might have wanted to explore, if the furious little black worry-mice hadn't been running around inside my head.

I should not have left him.

The convoy station was a tall, ramshackle affair, drips and rivulets working through its presswood ceiling and falling into a sad collection of slop-pots in every conceivable shape and size. Crowded, too, because a convoy—bellowing fourpads, shouting people, a collection of feral township youth selling snacks and small cheap things—had just arrived. It was the perfect time for me to infiltrate and blend, and it was also the perfect time for whoever had taken Geoff to exfiltrate.

Assuming I wasn't too late.

The corporate logo was a red globe on a blue background, not one I'd seen before. GeoNara. Pasted on everything, from the bleached buildings lining the thoroughfares to the sodden pieces of trash chucked into rusting cans. It took me less than two minutes to figure out the town was part of a mining and prospecting constellation, and that its last boom cycle had been a while ago. The veins for precious metals might be tapped out, but there were other layers in the strata around here that might be worth something.

Whoever took him was good. Damn good.

Agent good.

It was a fine time to wish I had some Agency backup. Running trace on someone in the middle of a desert is a thankless fucking task.

That was what I'd been counting on to help us. Probably what whoever snatched him was counting on too.

How didn't matter at this point. What mattered was finding out *who*. That would give me *where*, and when it did, they would see just how creative a flex liquidator could get at taking apart everything in her way. And if they'd hurt him . . .

. . . well. Best not to think about that just yet.

I drifted through the town in the heavy rain, sop-soaking and alert even though any onlooker would have sworn I was blind drunk. There were a few watchful predators, but none of them quite managed to catch up to me.

No breath of an agent in town. Nothing out of the ordinary. No encrypted commchatter, not a hair out of place. It was just a sleepy collection of out-City trash scrabbling away at surviving.

That was the biggest joke of all. No Ingress, and limited Egress, that was the rule with Cities. Couldn't let any contaminants in, and if you weren't on a sealed train who knew what you were carrying? The mystery was, why did so many people stay?

On the other hand, there was a whole collection of dreamers and scammers in-City who said *when I make Egress* as if it was something to look forward to. I could have told them outside wasn't any better than in, from what I could see. Still, if the Cities didn't want to lose plenty of their cheap workforce, the limits on Egress made sense.

Where is he?

I'd almost suspect a thopter had come down and whisked Geoff away. I'd torn apart every piece of gear, but there were no tracers in anything. No sign of a struggle, no sign of him. Just disappeared into thin air.

Someone *had* to have taken him. Sam, maybe? But where?

Doesn't matter. Going to find him.

Really, it was laughably simple. I crouched in an alley, the rain thrumming every surface around me, and ran over my plan once more.

Risky. Almost-stupid. Minimal chance of success.

All I had.

Okay, agent. Time to get arrested.

I got to work.

Corporations run townships differently than in-City enclaves. In a City, you've got the hub-belt—the Ring, where the skyscrapers rise and the security troops patrol—and the Ring suburbs where those who earn out or claw their way into corporate grace have their climate-controlled homes with little strips of genengineered monoculture weed masquerading as lawn. Then there's the Projekts where the industrial cogs rent their holes by the day or week, and the Cirquits where the heavy machinery throbs and the only thing left to fear is sliding even further down on the ladder because at least you don't live in the Slags.

The Projekts were rough, but the Slags were worse.

Corporation townships don't have Rings. They're only there for one thing: maximum efficiency in extracting cash or resources. Whatever doesn't serve that extraction doesn't get built. Nothing gets repaired, either, unless it'll improve that efficiency. Nobody survives unless there's a use for them.

All of which means one thing: the security offices have top-of-the-line gear; productivity requires the armored fist and the stat-rifle.

Also, it's easy to get hauled in, when you're in a corporation township. It can even be fun, if you like that sort of thing.

When you're looking to start a fight, you don't pick the biggest place—they deal with stopping chaos before it starts on a daily basis. You don't pick the smallest, either, because that won't make enough noise. You want the juicy center, the place just big enough to make a ruckus and small enough to overwhelm.

So I stamped into the middle-sized cantina, the one with a bead curtain that rattled every time someone came in, and the statfield was turned down all the way. No dust to keep out, not with all the water hanging in the air. Mud coated the peeling plas-lino floor, barely drying before boots smeared a fresh layer down. It was crammed with steaming warmbodies gulping down ersatz or grain alcohol before climbing back into the convoy transports, celebrating their safe arrival or imminent departure by poisoning themselves. Locals would be here to fleece the newcomers or get a bit of excitement, and the whole place was as crammed and blurry as only an afternoon of hard drinking could make it.

I shoved my way up to the bar, careful to bump into several of the warmbodies—not too hard, but not too softly either. The mood in here was just right, a desperate, bleary fermenting, nerves not as sodden as they would be later but inhibitions nicely blunted.

Wet and draggled as I was, nobody paid me a second glance except those I stepped on during my trip to the bar.

It's always easy to start a fight. All you have to do is spill someone's drink.

I jostled a big bear of a man—probably a mechanic, carrying a powerful fug of lubricant, sweat, and burning metal—with just enough force to slop his glass of grain alcohol. He growled an obscenity, but he didn't have enough dominance in him to start a melee. Still, I trod on his toes as I staggered past, all the warmbodies now marking me as drunk and witless.

By the time I'd made a complete circuit of the cantina's main floor, I'd antagonized just about everyone who was likely to have a temper. That wasn't what had the whole place on edge, though.

It was the carefully balanced pheromone mist I was pumping out, saturating the warmbodies with uneasy aggression. The roar of conversation had turned saw-edged, but the bartender—only about half as intelligent as Madam B back in New Vega, with the vicious green eye of a looksee implemented on his withered left shoulder—was too busy mixing and pouring to notice.

Walls of glazed mud, shored into place with pressed pulp-fibre and scrap, dripped with condensation as dusk rose and the temperature dropped. I waited just a little longer, letting the pheromone mist work and take on a darker, sharper edge.

A knot of caravaneers loudly but genially arguing over some arcane bit of trivia at one end of the bar didn't notice when I sidled nearby. Twenty seconds of fine-tuning the mist, hearing the pitch and timbre of the argument change, and I struck, all but throwing myself against the biggest of them. His cornglass mug went flying, grain alcohol spilled, and he bellowed, lashing out.

From there it was simple. Feinting and ducking, blurring to different flashpoints in the crowd, adding just enough pressure to keep everything boiling. I even helpfully threw one or two of the warmbodies who tried to restore order out through the bead curtain into a sea of gritty mud.

By the time the security detail arrived with shock batons to sort everything out, the entire cantina was a shambles, the bartender cowering in the only shelter he could find—the malodorous pit they charitably called a restroom. It was no great trick to get shocked or cuffed, I just had to go rigid before going limp, and pretend that it hurt. They assumed I was just another caravaneer, and within fifteen minutes I was stat-locked in a cell hollowed out of crumbling sandstone, in the basement of the security detail's nerve center.

Just where I wanted to be.

* * *

The head of security was a hard-bellied male warmbody with white muttonchop whiskers and a shiny fist-shaped alloy badge. The blue and red of his uniform had only faded a little, and the rest of his salt-and-pepper mane was slicked back with rancid fat mixed with cheap synthesized cologne.

The shockflex restraints at my wrists hummed slightly as I shifted my weight. Rolled in mud and splattered with both ersatz and grain alcohol, no doubt I looked sorry indeed. I'd heard them taking out the flotsam of the fight in ones and twos for a couple hours now, sorting through the mess now that everyone was reasonably sober.

The nameplate on the desk read *Berry*, its mellow brass gleam no doubt lovingly polished every week. The lino was glossy, though it had been patched in places. Leaning back in his dangerously creaking chair, the big man in town regarded me from top to toe.

The door closed. Subroutines over every autonomic. They had security measures, yes. But all the scanhops, triggervalves, pressure sensors, and bioscanners in the world won't help when they're not even switched on.

Too easy. I dispelled impatience, settled into waiting.

My awareness roved in wide arcs as the chair creaked. There was the terminal, sitting dead and dark. After so long in the damn desert it was a relief to see a rectangular black block with fitted input jacks and a pair of split keyboards. Looked like a PransTech 5806, not the newest but not entirely obsolete either. It would have linkup capability, and once I—

"Ain't you a pretty little thing." The warmbody heaved himself up. His chair grunted. I had to replay the audio inside my head just to make sure he'd actually said that.

I'm covered in mud and stink of fourpad and stale alcohol. Your oculars need adjusting, sir. All the same, it made everything simpler. Once again, a warmbody sank to the lowest possible level.

Was there ever a time when they didn't? After a while, when you're so thoroughly implemented, you sort of . . . forget.

"You ain't got no ID, and no multipass either. So. What's your name, honey?"

I peered through filthy, matted strings of hair. The restraints at my wrists were stupid-simple flexcable with low shock capability. Easy. The warmbody was taller and probably thought he was heavier than me, and was most likely used to the desperate offering whatever they could. Good thing my gear was safely hidden.

You thought Geoff was safely hidden too.

That was a distracting thought. I shelved it and let the warmbody heave himself a little closer.

"Now, you don't look like you like being dirty. You tell me your name, and we'll get you a nice bath. Hot water. Wouldn't you like that?"

I wondered how many times he'd said this to any female without ID unlucky enough to end up in one of the sandstone cells. I wondered how long ago was the first time he'd said it. So far, this was depressingly textbook.

He was almost in range.

What's that? Footsteps. Running. My hormone balance shifted, my weight sinking into my left leg. If they'd scanned me—but I'd have *felt* it.

Like you didn't feel someone watching you and your kid? Move. Move now.

I didn't, though. A runner's instinct, keeping me loose and ready because he was still just out of optimal strikezone. There was a thudding at the door.

"Berry!" It was the same pimple-faced guard who had prodded me out of my cell. "Attack!"

"For the love of—"

The guard started babbling, something about bodies out at the Shalter place. "Everything busted up and there's—you ain't gonna believe this, Sheriff, but there's *blood*, throats torn open and everything. Whatever did it drank their blood."

The muttonchopped disaster stepped squarely into the strike zone, and I *moved.*

Kick to the side, the pimpled guard's knee cracking like a twig, and the flexcable of the restraints groaned as I looped it around Berry's neck. The shock capability tingled pleasantly across my buffering, but turned the warmbody into a jitterlocked piece of meat. A quick yank to keep it snug, another precise application of force to the guard's solar plexus with my other foot. Just like dancing, not even quarter-speed.

Creaking as the small bones in Berry's neck fractured. He kicked as the shocks jolted through him, but it was child's play to keep him from regaining his balance, and motor function degrades almost instantly when the carotid is clamped anyway. I wouldn't have saved him for Geoff, though—an acidic note to his sweat shouted some form of *disease.*

I didn't have time to slowly strangle him, so I gave another quick jerk, cleanly fracturing the cervicals, and let his body spill to the floor. Dragged the gasping, kitten-weak pimple-guard further into the room by his ankle, and heaved the reinforced door shut, priming the pressure sensors on the keypad with a quick tap.

I didn't want to be disturbed.

The sheriff's bowels had released. It didn't matter, but I did drag the guard away from the mess. The terminal lit up when I pressed the corekey; the spectral light from the four screens—only four, this was the desert—bathing the entire room in a harsher glow.

What I wouldn't give for a nice KanthCoroCorp deck. Oh well. Adapt and make do, agent.

"Here we go," I muttered, more to give the guard something to focus on than out of any real need to be audible. His gasping and the irregularity in his heartbeat would need to be dealt with soon, because I wanted him conscious enough to question.

Whatever did it drank their blood. My fingers danced over the split keyboards, splitting queries and narrowing down options. The linkup wasn't even password protected.

Idiots.

The guard's hitching breaths smoothed a little. "Berry," he moaned. "*Berry . . .*"

Shock. I'd have to question him soon.

First, though, there was hacking to do.

"The Shalter place" was a slumshack on the very periphery of Carsona, surrounded by piles of slagorra that steamed under the rain. The stuff—byproduct of producing the heavy elements for fuelcores and other indispensible tech—sent shivers over my skin, even buffered. It was a good thing the nanos made sure you didn't get gene-fraying from the stuff. Slag was element-rich in its own right, but working with the stuff meant you had to replace your labor every couple years. The mutations just get too bad, and once the worst of it sets in the skin starts splitting and liquefied stuff that used to be warmbody comes trickling out.

There was no cordon yet. Without the late lamented Berry to bark orders, there was time before someone sorted things out, went above their paygrade, and actually started trying to untangle what had happened.

Not that they'd ever find Berry's body. His replacement was

likely to be just as loathsome, but that wasn't my problem. Neither were the other security personnel I'd disposed of at headquarters, more as an afterthought than anything else.

Might as well be tidy, if I was going to cause chaos in this backass burg as well as New Vega. There's no reason to ever be sloppy or haphazard.

I toed open the pressboard door and slid inside, exhaling softly.

Bodies flung everywhere. The throats were savaged, almost torn free. Splatters of arterial spray—relief and fresh unease warred uneasily inside my savagely controlled autonomics. Geoff didn't tear, he made neat little wounds and drank until he was finished, just like a good little boy should.

Not nearly enough blood. Multiple attackers. Look at that, too—stat-burns. Starlike pattern. Shit. CoreTech weaponry. I wonder—

I didn't even get a chance to finish the thought. A betraying creak as weight shifted, and a long lean shape landed on the bloodsoaked flooring. I almost, *almost* struck, but ended up giving just a betraying little twitch before I recognized him.

Sam, his wheat-gold hair damp and disarranged, actually *glared* at me. "Will you quit doing that? I'm here to *help*."

"I left your head in the room," I pointed out, spinning down from redline with a purely internal sigh. "What more do you want?"

He brushed aside my generosity with a single, efficient hand-wave. "We have to jump, Jess. Where's the kid?"

Which answered one question, maybe. I crouched, keeping Sam in my peripheral as I examined a small, crumpled body. Slag distortions had given the little girl extra fingers and turned her face into a runneled mass, but her spincotton frock had been clean before death visited, and a short scan revealed no malnutrition markers on her bones or in her slagtouched flesh.

Even the slagged sometimes care for their spawn.

Sam was twitchier than I'd ever seen him. "Jess? Where is he?"

"Not gonna tell *you*, Sam. Shut up." *Let me think.*

"I want to help, Jess. Someone else wants to help you too."

"Oh?" I touched a piece of un-split flesh on the small corpse, chemtesting filling me with information, and temperature scans all returning different answers. *If you pitch me about the Agency now and promise me all will be forgiven, I'll kill you for good. I might even enjoy it.* "Who's that?"

I expected him to say anything other than what came out of his implemented mouth. Sam bent down to pick up a long, sharp-ended piece of slag alloy. "John Nikor, Jess. Who else?"

I looked up at him, my hair slicked back with mud and rain, and I'll admit it.

I actually laughed.

CHAPTER SEVEN

MYTH

I hadn't laughed like that since . . . well, since far before I was implemented. The Projekts beats any hilarity out of you soon enough.

My handler regarded me with a patient, pained expression just two shades away from his usual *just passing the message along, agent* blandness. It was the same look he wore when telling me damage tallies were going to be added to my debt. He glanced at the walls, probably collating all the information I'd already gleaned from the bloodspatter and starbursts of scorching characteristic of CoreTech weaponry—it was enough to make me wonder if they'd taken Geoff again. Slivers of bone driven into the pressboard walls like shrapnel, too.

Definitely not Geoff. But not enough blood, either. Throats shredded postmortem in most cases, to hide what?

The silence turned elastic. He kept watching me. I kept examining the corpses. *That's three attackers. Four—wait, more than that. Trained, but they didn't take this place apart like a raid team would. This was something else.* "Yeah, the hero of the Gene Wars is going to swoop in and save us. John Nikor's a myth, Sam. Just like the Collective, fairies, and buttercups."

"So is your little boy. There's not enough blood here."

You're just now noticing? "He didn't do this." My unease sharpened, a piece of the puzzle falling into place with a click. The Collective—*that* particular little fable was what I'd been trying to remember since the agents with their silver-sheen eyes, but I just filed it away for further thinking. My bandwidth needed to be spent on the here-and-now.

Sam's thoughtful nod could have been mistaken for a twitch. "That's CoreTech weaponry. Looks like they replicated some parts of the process."

"The process." *Come on, give me something to work with.*

"Where is he, Jess?" Sam stopped, giving me a thorough scan, and I winced a little internally. It wasn't like I could hide it forever, though. "Oh, *shit*. You've lost him."

"Now would be a good time for you to come clean, Sammy." I couldn't even feel happy that he was sticking to audible.

"Do you know who took him?" The rain outside slackened a bit, slightly less deafening. Curtains of it, slamming into the mud, and it would run off before it could do any good to this thirsty, starving place.

"Working on it." Still, it was vaguely cheering to think maybe Sam—and by extension, the Agency—might consider me an asset to be retained. A little backup would be nice, especially now that I'd basically sent out a floating blue-neon Cirquit billboard. The risk would be enough to send me hightailing back into the desert, if not for the prospect of seeing which fish rose to the bait. I could leverage the ensuing fracas to find out who'd taken Geoff.

One way or another.

Sam's autonomics didn't budge. "I can bring you in. Offer's still good."

I tilted my head fractionally. Never taking the first offer is good tactics. "Don't insult my intelligence. The Agency's not very forgiving."

"Not Agency. Weren't you listening? Nikor, Jess. The legend himself. The Rebellion's always looking for disaffected agents."

You expect me to believe that pile of fourpad shit? "Don't have time for holoserials and fairytales." *Too quiet. I don't like this.* Nothing on my scans, but still, my hackles were up.

Even the most intrusive implementation leaves a space for instinct. I'd crouched near the little girl in the spincotton frock, my balance shifting as autonomics slid into subtly altered patterns. The nanos responded, prepping me for combat. Hormones shifting, brain glucose uptake spiking hard, enhanced muscles primed for action.

And Sam noticed. He switched to subvocal. *"I don't hear anything."*

Of course he didn't. There was nothing to hear.

Consequently, when they blasted through the wall with CoreTech plasilca-film explosive, they knocked him down.

But not me.

Fast. Implemented-fast, but no commchatter and they weren't buffered. Stunprobes crackled, a statbolt whined past, and I kicked the one looming over Sam's prone body. Heavy, but not agent-heavy, the male—tall, a shock of floppy dark hair with chips of something pale in its long flow clacking as he flew—curled around the force of the kick and collided with a blond male in standard-issue City shocktroop wear. Deep navy to blend with shadowed corners, plasleather worn to suppleness, loaded with weapon straps, for a moment I was in-City again, and this was just the same as every other liquidation of a high-value target carried out in alleys, cheap Cirquit rooms, or corporate highrises.

One hit me from the side with a whip-flexing shockprobe,

a starburst of tooth-gritting clampdown before my buffering shunted the crackle of stat aside. Feedback through a few intake channels, a brief squeal ignored out of habit. A shockprobe will reduce a warmbody without buffergear to seizures and pants-pissing on its mildest setting, but even dialed all the way up they're only a minor annoyance to a liquidator.

The pressboard wall shuddered as I used momentum from the one who hit me to crash into another, my hand tangling in straps and giving a quick jerk. He spun away, smashing into the wall again. The entire structure groaned. We'd have the place broken down to the slag in no time, at this rate.

Move. Staying still would give them an advantage. One of them had a statrifle unlimbered, and the whine of recharge peaked just before I dropped and rolled again, the plasilca knife I'd plucked from my first target singing a high stressnote as a flash scoured the inside of the shack. Thick ozone reek, the stat-bolt splatting on the wall and scorching a familiar starshape.

Decisions, decisions. Did I keep them away from Sam, or hope they would mistake him for a threat? I knew which one it was, and the sharp burst of irritation was there and gone in a flash, not useful and therefore ignored. *Oh, for the love of—*

I was already committed, the plasilca knife shrieking as it whip-bent and my hand darted down, opening the blond's femoral artery and flashing back up, severing what I could in the inguinal fold with a vicious twist as I pushed off again, just barely dodging another darkhaired male whose face was a rictus. His strike went wide, lips skinned back from his teeth, and if I hadn't been so busy dodging another crackle-hissing statbolt I might have been startled by the shape of his swollen canines.

What the—

As it was, I dropped and rolled again, ending neatly on my feet and pushing off with all the force enhanced muscles could give me, colliding in midair with the first floppy-haired bastard. The bits of gleaming in his hair were bleached bone, knotted into the strands with spincotton, clacking as he growled at me.

The sound-profile was strange, but I didn't have time for more than record-and-flag because we were both airborne. Force transferred, one hand in his hair, I dragged the plasilca blade across his throat and *shoved.* Arterial spray splattered, I landed hard, the floor cracking. Noisome dust puffed up, my hair full of splinters. Skewers of pressboard jagging up, another statbolt whined, and a short grunt of effort punctuated the chaos as I wiped the third's legs from underneath him, my palm threatening to slide on damp blood-greased pressboard before I gained my feet again with a convulsive movement. *Where's the last? Dammit, they're quiet. Not even a pulse until they're right on top of you.*

The third, squat and corded with muscle, hissed as he fell. Another strange sound, but I didn't have time to think about it. So fucking *fast,* implemented reflexes straining to keep up.

If he hadn't been sloppy, new to the enhanced speed of his limbs, he might have hurt me. As it was, I got a good fistful of his hair and surged *up*, legs flying loose. My right heel brushed the ceiling, I had enough height and *twisted* as I dropped, dragging his head in ways no cervical structure could support. A short sharp crack, my feet thudding down on sagging pressboard, a rain-soaked burst of air through the hole in the wall mixing with the stink of blood, stat-scorch, death, and slag.

Extending in a lunge, the fourth shocktrooper tracking me with the rifle's muzzle. *This is going to sting.* Calculating the intervals—he would get off a shot, I was too far away. Where was Sam? Was he still stunned? Facilitators weren't as durable as liquidators, they were built for—

Crack. The rifle clattered to the floor, and Sam stepped aside, almost mincingly. The dripping point of an alloy bar thrust out of the fourth man's chest, and I had time to study his graying face as shock took over and he fell with a shack-shaking thud.

I dove for the CoreTech statrifle, grabbing the strap before it hit the floor. Sam shook his head. Blood and dust grimed onto his face, his eyes blazing and a chilling little smile on his lips, he didn't seem the same facilitator I'd been getting my marching orders from for years.

"So that's how it is." He toed the body of the fourth shock-trooper. "Great."

What? I didn't bother asking. He was talking about Nikor and getting cryptic. Maybe a cognitive degrade? I had dumped him in caustic sludge. Maybe some had worked its way into his cerebellum.

Of course, I was halfway to believing fairytales were coming to life myself.

I eased my way across shattered flooring, trying to avoid the strewn ruins of slagged warmbodies. I sank into a crouch next to the blond. Blood spread sluggishly from his slashed thigh, but not nearly enough. *Huh.*

"Jess?" A new note to Sam's voice. What was it? Didn't matter.

I sniffed, tasted the air. The copper of fresh blood was somehow *off.* I touched a fingertip to the blond's leg, reflexive chemtesting returning a series of answers that made no sense at all. The edges of the slice up his thigh quivered oddly. I'd cut almost down to bone, laying open the artery. He should have bled out in seconds.

"Jess, I'd get away from that if I were you."

I ignored Sam again. Used my thumb to pry up the blond's upper lip. *Canines, retractable—see the pouch there? Musculature changes there and there. Modified jaw structure—must hurt like hell to have that clamp down. Interesting. Geoff's are neater, though. This is just a sloppy copy.* "These guys are too fast," I murmured. "Too strong. No implementation, but they *have* to be implemented. Unless . . ."

"Yeah, you're looking at CoreTech's second-gens. Didn't think they'd let them out-City, but they must be desperate."

"Mh." A noncommittal noise. *Keep talking. Second-gens?* Was Geoff the first generation? Or a later one, refined? Perfected?

The later generation of *what*, though? Shocktroops that didn't need implementation, probably. But if they had these assholes primed and ready for exploitation in the relatively short time I'd been outside the City, that rather radically changed the shape of the playing-board. Still, the scramble to retain Geoff wouldn't make sense unless the process wasn't perfected yet and they consequently needed the iteration he represented, whether earlier or later.

The edges of the thigh-wound quivered a little more, flushing rosy even in the dimness. There was a creaking crackle from across the room—just like nanos fusing cervicals together.

The blond's cheek twitched.

"Jess." Very calmly, and very quietly, Sam took a step towards me. "I really think we should both get out of here now."

I think you're half right. I uncoiled, my weight balanced throughout the entire motion. The only corpses that weren't twitching were the slagged warmbodies, and the one Sam had pinned with a slag-alloy bar. "You go ahead."

"You have no idea what these guys are capable of."

"And you do? Either start talking or get the fuck out of here." I inhaled smoothly, brought the statrifle up to my shoulder. Now was a fine time to wish I'd stopped to get my cached gear on my way from the security headquarters. "Because these motherfuckers have information, and I want it."

"I can give you answers. I'd love to. We just should really get out of here."

"Go on, then." The statrifle's whine settled into the ultrasonic of a full charge, and I quit listening to it.

He sighed. "You were never this much trouble in-City."

"Maybe you just weren't paying attention."

"Believe me, I was. Jess, *please*."

The creaking sounds intensified. I tilted my head slightly, scanning. They were damn near invisible to infrared, even though they bled hot. No scars on their chins, but modified teeth, jaws, musculature. Fast and pretty indestructible.

Well, maybe not *indestructible*. But still, this kicked implementation right where it hurt. So why would a corporation release them into the wild like this?

Maybe they weren't released.

I needed a few cycles to rest. I needed to think this through. I needed to find Geoff. What were the chances of these enhanced warmbodies serving that last overriding purpose?

More twitching. More creaking. More crackling.

"Jess." Firmly, now. "I don't want to have to drag you out of here."

"As if you could." I racked the statrifle, the descending throb of its powering down sending a ripple up my back. I glanced at the hole in the wall, and decided it was as good a direction as any to make an exit.

If Sam was smart, he'd follow.

Just behind the crest of a slag-heap, I hunched my shoulders and watched the activity below. Warmbodies swarmed the site, two or three in ancient containment suits. Hauling the bodies out, picking over the belongings—a scuffle broke out a few rags of clothing, but all in all, it was a quiet affair.

Only one of the shocktroopers was carried out—the one with the alloy spike through his chest. Did they leave the rest of the bastards in there? Impossible, there was good gear to scavenge.

Sam, next to me, was motionless as only an agent could be. He observed a safe distance, though, and lay at an angle that would give him a moment's worth of warning if I twitched in his direction. Whether it was caution or distaste, I wasn't going to guess.

"They're looking for him too." Not subaudible, no reason to grumble when the warmbodies were so far away. "Or at least, they were. Agency just knows I was dumped in a vat, not that you had anything to do with it; Core and Niful bid for two HK teams but didn't want Control knowing *anything* about the kid. I've fudged the reports as much as I'm able. As far as Control knows, you're a casualty too. Tied off, game over."

They still weren't bringing the shocktroopers out. The security troops—the half-dozen or so who had been out of the headquarters while I was there—didn't look uneasy. They didn't have a cordon set up.

It was a puzzle.

"You could thank me." Sam moved just a little, cycling muscles to keep them ready. "Or say you're happy to see me now."

Look at that. I'm well past my tadpole years and implemented to the max, and yet I still feel like rolling my eyes. The swarming died down. Nobody wants to stay near slag any longer than they can help it. What would it be like to live in it? Breathe it in?

At least the desert was cleaner, somehow. Or maybe it just seemed that way.

"Jess?"

"Shut up," I said, curt and soft. He had *never* been this chatty before. No wonder he was in facilitating, if he couldn't keep his mouth shut. I was beginning to wish we were in-City again.

Not really.

The warmbodies trickled away. I waited. It was a good thing I wasn't too attached to this spincotton frock—what little of it was left after the past twelve hours would have to go in a furnace.

Even chemshower won't get slag out. At this point I was wearing more mud than fabric. The rain had slacked still further, and thin traceries of steam rose from my skin before the nanos readjusted camouflage mode.

Just wait. Even though I could talk myself into going back down there and ripping up the floorboards, I stayed put. Enhanced healing—did they feel pain? If they did, sooner or later one of them would break and tell me everything I wanted to know.

Torture's unreliable, though. They might just tell you what they think you want to know.

Often, the quickest way to what you want is just waiting. Even fully implemented agents sometimes fail to grasp that simple fact.

Respiration slowing. Cycling through my own muscles, so softly, so patiently.

Where is he? Are they feeding him? Will anyone kiss him goodnight? Listen to him breathing during the day? Is he all right? Little worry-mice running around inside my almost-invulnerable brain. Just because you can pop a subroutine over the autonomics doesn't mean the feelings go away.

Yet another thing I wished they would have told me before implementation. It wouldn't have made any difference, but still.

Dark smears, oozing free of the shack's dim bulk. They didn't move like warmbodies, or like agents. They slid along as if greased, silent as death.

Only not quite. Three shadows, and an *unsound.* It didn't register on intakes, it didn't lend itself to a profile. It hit behind the ear, in the place where a tickle tells you it's going to rain, or that a particular rooftop run or corporate war is about to get ugly.

That's how you hunt them, then. My autonomics clamped down, and the dark smears blurred up the slag-choked path towards the low punky glow that was Carsona. Moving in standard raid formation, you could see the corpsec training all over them.

So what do you think they're going to do?

I thought about it, and looked at Sam. "They weren't born like that." Hushed, conspiratorial, five little audible words.

He shook his head. The rain had plastered his hair down, darkened it. A wet gleam from his eyes, and a little heat bleeding off both of us now in steam-trails. "No. They weren't."

We weren't born like this, either. I ran over everything inside my head again. The eastern rim of the world would soon be on fire. A warmbody wouldn't see dawn approaching, but I did.

And so would they.

"You're a facilitator." I stretched, a little gingerly, and stood up. Mud splatted free, the skywater more a mist with pretensions than an actual rain at this point.

"I wasn't always." His throat moved as he swallowed, looking over my shoulder at the town's nacreous glow.

Are you sure? But maybe he could have meant he wasn't always implemented. Maybe we'd both been thinking the same thing.

"You're going to tell me about them." My hands loose, my subroutines all even. "Then I'm going to find my kid."

"*We're* going to find your kid."

"Maybe."

"Maybe? You're going to dump me somewhere else?"

"That part," I told him, "depends on what your fairytale wants with him."

I stripped off the slag-steaming rags on the way; the chem-shower was ancient and rickety but it worked just fine. There was no actual water, but it didn't matter—slag sometimes burns if you add H2O, no reason to make the nanos repair that too. Especially since I hadn't had a good solar charge in a few days, and expended serious effort on the shocktroopers.

Wandering naked through a corporation town at dawn gives

you time to think. I checked my internal chrono, wincing at how much time had passed. Staying here was a fool's game, but leaving meant I wouldn't be able to watch who came scrambling to the table and deduce who'd taken Geoff.

Collecting my gear was Sam's job, and it was there when I got out of the chemshower. For a moment we were in-City again, the facilitator standing guard while the agent cleaned up, the mission moving into another phase or the prearranged break drawing closer.

There wasn't a bed in this sorry shack of a room, but at least it wasn't slagged. Just a pressboard cube atop one of the smaller liveries, smelling of fourpad and a deeper, gassy, warmbody reek as well. The rain would have brought up whatever sewage wasn't fully desiccated yet.

I ran my fingers through my damp hair, tugging at tangles. I'd had this sleek bob for years, but I was wondering if I should grow it out a bit to match the majority of warmbody women in the Waste. "Start at the beginning."

"CoreTech's scrambling. Their project's gone sideways."

Again, I didn't roll my eyes. I decided on a spincotton shift and pair of denims bought for hard credit in New Vega. I *did* give Sam a single eloquent glance.

He must have felt it, even though he didn't turn around. "Or psychotic, your choice. The second-gens have slipped their leash and gone hunting."

"Hunting Geoff?"

"Oh, it's *Geoff* now?" He sighed, peering out the window past a sunbleached rag of drapery. "Actually, I don't think so. I think they're just thirsty."

Thirsty. "My kid's first-gen?"

"No, the first gens died off. Something about anaphylactic shock and unfiltered sun-radiation. Your kid's the zero. A metagenius built him, but a few days after decanting the builder was found with a hole in his head and a suicide note."

Interesting. A quick scan of my saddlebags. I wondered if I'd be able to pick up the fourpads again, especially the one who liked to eat my hair. He made an odd gurgle-snort sound when something surprised him, and his loping pace was easier than any other fourpad's was likely to be.

That's the trouble with spending time with warmbody things for any length of time. You can try not to get attached, but it doesn't work.

"Who did the metagenius work for?" There were no little pops or pings in the saddlebags. Maybe Sam intended to keep me in visual range.

Sam let out a soft breath, and there was a whine in a range I knew all too well. "Jess . . ."

Uh-oh.

I suppose it was only fair. After all, I'd rammed a lectricprobe through him, and later torn his head off. To his credit, though, it didn't hurt. The statpistol, dialed up to max, stunned me for a few precious seconds, but that was enough for him to pop the sticky silico-stretchy numbpatch onto my bare arm. They're counted and recounted, only signed out with two authorized Control representatives present, doled out grudgingly, and almost never allowed out into the field.

It didn't matter where he got it. The point was, I went down *hard*, everything in me shrieking as the nanos decoded the chemsignal—*time to protect the host by shutting down consciousness*, the same tingling and flood of warmth as sinking into the restraint tank for upgrades, fighting it, fighting it, no use.

Blackness. Gone.

CHAPTER EIGHT

AGENT WARFARE

Coming up from a numbpatch is always the same. Like dawn, a thin crack of gray at the very edge of the world, the nanos getting the signal to bring you back online. You don't ever dream in that black bleakness. Still, sometimes, on the razor margin between chem-induced haze and the hurtful clarity of waking, a brief burst of REM gets through.

Sliding across gritty concrete on my knees, the knifeblade dulled so it didn't flash under the assault of neon, drag against the blade as it parted flesh. Sudden hot reek of gutsplit as I dropped the fucker looking to dust me, a wave of projectile ammo overhead—Sixty Bill's cadre were cleaning an avenue, and getting me caught in the crossfire was just a bonus. Which was why I'd picked this route across the top edge of the Sixty's territory, if I went fast enough the flying bullets would stitch a line into the rooftop behind me.

Unfortunately, a couple runners thought they'd drop me en route and take the cargo. Pounds and pounds of sugar-vox weighing me down, ready to be turned into caprasan when I got to the dropoff. The caprasan would be sold in smidges for hard credit or untraceable bit, getting the corporate drones high as shit and letting them forget for a few minutes the drudgery of being owned.

On my feet now, skipping sideways, two more runners closing in from my right and the pick-pock-pock of projectiles on my heels, and one of the runners had a shockstick. It sputtered in the gloaming, a bright stuttering-white flash, probably how Sixty's crew were tracking us all, and I took the only way out—over the side of the building, freefall, tumbling and hoping the heavy-duty spincotton awning was still where it had been a day ago when I scoped the route.

Hit hard, it gave resiliently, and my weak little warmbody curled around itself and pushed off, kinetic energy transferred, just enough force—

Hit, hard, breaking glass and blood flying as I rolled, too high on adrenaline and motion to feel the sutures I'd need later. The fat payday at the end of my route had a slice taken off for medical—by the time I made it to the dropoff I'd lost a lot of blood—but it wasn't bad at all.

Still, it wasn't quite enough. It never was.

The lase-sutures were barely in before I realized what I had to do. They stung, but I turned down the expensive shot of torvane to block the pain and limped home. Had to face up to it: I was getting slow, and by the time I saved up enough, the growing flesh-anchor in my womb would be more expensive to get rid of than even the best runner in the City could afford.

That night, my heart a clot in my throat and dried blood still crackling in my clothes, I started planning.

Smell of smoke—a campfire, not the carcinogen reek of civilization. I lay very still, scanning through systems, collating. Warmbodies can get hangovers from grain alcohol, agents get the aftermath of numbpatches. I tested fingers and toes, scanned for anything implanted while I was out. Everything the way it should be, organ functions tiptop, nanos buzzing about their business.

Buffered heartbeat. An unfamiliar rasping. Charring—no, meat cooking. Fat dripping from flesh, spattering in open flames. A tuneless whistle, air pushed out through lips, occasionally following the track of a pop ditty or two popular in-City a few weeks ago.

The consideration that I could lunge across the fire and damage him swam into view. I considered it, set it aside. Scanning revealed we were far away from anything even approximating a township. The water table had risen even more, and I could barely catch a thrumming of worms in the distance.

He'd taken me out of Carsona. Great.

Everything seemed to be functioning properly. I pushed myself up on my elbows. He must have taken the numbpatch off a good half-hour ago. It takes a while for it to flush out of your system when the nanos are groggy.

How long was I out? Fortunately, numbpatches don't interfere with chrono. Twelve hours, give or take. The rock here was still crumbling sandy stone, but it exhaled a bit of leftover moisture. The humidity had plummeted, barometric pressure was back to what it had been before the rain swept through, and the furnace glow of a bloody sunset was dying in the west. It wasn't quite a cave, the ceiling only halfway covering a sandy floor scattered with chunks of fallen rock. Still, the remaining bits of it scanned solid enough.

The urge to yawn rose up, was ruthlessly repressed. A stupid warmbody reflex, I had all the oxygen I needed.

Sam crouched on the other side of a small fire, staring at the small skinned animal on a makeshift spit. His hair had bleached itself out under the fierce assault of sun, but his skin had darkened to drag in all the solar it could. Hunched down like that, he looked uncomfortably like Geoff. Males lack the hip width to really be comfortable in that position; they always look like incorrectly folded origami.

"You're probably furious," he said, quietly.

Gee, how could you guess? I pushed myself up to my feet. The nanos began system-flushing numbing-waste, tuning muscles and organs back into a well-ordered symphony instead of a dozing beast. Stretched my arms out, tested my legs. "Slip anything under my skin?"

"It's a facilitator's job to care for the agent, and to keep the agent from going off the psychological rails." Chapter and verse. He blinked, thermascanning the meat. "You need calories."

I could have had solar if you hadn't numbed me. Useless. A more thorough scan of the area turned up a few fourpads, tucked around a fold of stone and cropping at spiny succulents. My gear was in a neat pile, and the angle of the shadows gave me a rough idea of where Carsona would be. "See you."

"Where are you headed?"

"Carsona."

"What the fuck *for,* Jess? I just got you out of there."

"Thanks." I couldn't have sounded any less grateful if I'd tried. "By the time I get back there the place will be crawling, which is just what I wanted. If you stay out of the way you might even learn something."

He was quick. Glanced up at me, bleached eyes narrowed slightly. "What did you do?"

"Used their uplink to throw a few hack-bombs. Everyone who has an interest in my kid is going to rub elbows and confuse each other."

A thoughtful nod, then his chin sank as he worked through the strategy inside his own head. "Except whoever took him. Not your usual delicate touch, Jess."

When dealing with idiots, any blunt instrument will do. I swallowed the urge to tell him to go fuck himself, stretched a little more, and headed for my gear. He'd even taken my boots off. Sand gritted underfoot, still warm. Hotter, in fact, than a warmbody would find comfortable.

"Will you stop? You need calories. Whoever took the kid is long gone. Let's make sure you don't join him."

"Touching." Peeling aside canvas and leather flaps, I dug in the bags. At top speed, I could probably make Carsona before dawn. The whole place would probably be alive with dug-in hostiles.

A whole transport-load of fun just waiting for me.

Sam's tone was losing its blandness. He was no longer just reporting the news. "Look, I got you involved in this. I'll get you out, but you have to stop—"

The look I gave him shut him up so quickly he probably almost lost a chunk of his self-healing tongue. "You have two choices, Sammy Facilitator. Help, or get gone. Both are dependent upon you getting rid of the idea that you're in control of anything to do with me *or* my kid."

Maybe he decided discretion would get him further than fucking with me, because he studied the meat over the fire as if it had started twitching again. My weapons seemed fine, the holsters didn't appear to have any telltales in them. Fully suited, I knocked my boots clean and tugged them on, took a deep breath, and began weighing the advisability of taking a fourpad.

I could move faster, for longer, without.

In the middle of that decision, an odd sound fuzzed through my aurals. Long and drawn-out, a high ululating cry a few klicks to the southwest.

Another answered from due north. I sniffed, cautiously,

but the wind was wrong. At the very edge of scanrange, weird shadows made no sense until I realized Sam had brought me to the end of the desert. There were *trees* in the distance, or something so like them it made no difference.

The cries rose and fell, a harmony too harsh for warmbody throats. The spikes and valleys separated into unique voices. Whatever they were, they were singing.

"Do you know what that is?" He pulled the meat off the fire. "Can you guess?"

Pebbles shifting, sand moving. I tensed, but it wasn't Sam. I crouched, compressing myself, ready to spring. *What the fuck is that? I hear movement, but nothing—*

More long trilling cries, long drawn-out cathedrals of rough melody that tried to raise the fine hairs all over me. Autonomic control tightened, and a picture flashed inside my head. Shaggy shoulders, long snouts, ivory teeth, and expressive eyes ringed with gold, reflecting oddly at night.

Even in-City, we had dogs. They even howl. But everything outside the walls is stronger. Sharper. Unfiltered.

More intense.

"Wolves," I breathed. *I'm actually hearing wolves.* Fairytales, myths, and fables were coming out of the walls.

The stealthy sounds intensified, but I wasn't ready for it. It resolved out of the leaping shadows at the edge of the firelight, and for a split second I thought it was one of them. A shaggy four-legged shape, bonecracking jaws and padded feet, long swaying fur—all the implementation in the world can't erase an atavistic thrill when another hunter shows its teeth the first time.

But it wasn't a wolf. Dusk swirled away, the hard sharp diamond stars poking through the velvet holding up a strengthening bone-colored moon, and I thought the numbing had come back because all the strength ran out of my arms and legs. For the first time since I'd been dumped out of a restraint vat to try my new, incredibly strong, incredibly resilient limbs, I staggered.

He threw himself into my arms. *"Abbymom! Abbymom! Mom! Mom!"* Piercing cries, but I couldn't answer.

I didn't have the breath.

"I woke up!" His face was alight with excitement, pride, glee. All but bubbling with delight. "I woke up and you weren't there, and I thought—"

"I went to check on . . ." I had to ease up, I was squeezing him too tightly. "All our gear was there, Geoff! How the *hell* did you wander off?"

"I didn't. I was *below*, it's the first time it happened. They . . ." A quick flicker of his tongue, wetting pale lips. He needed fluids soon. His eyes danced, and he hadn't lost weight at all. "Well, *they* helped. Told me you didn't know."

"They?" I shook my head when he opened his mouth to explain, and I couldn't stop smoothing his cheeks, touching his dark hair. Sand all over him, and you could tell he hadn't bathed—a healthy heat-haze hung on him, filling my receptors with absolute proof he was alive, and whole, and safe. "No. Listen to me. You could have been hurt. You could have been *killed*."

"I was fine." The scar on his chin quivered a little. "I just went *below*."

"Want something to eat?" Sam hadn't moved. Still crouched on the other side of the small fire, he was very pointedly *not* studying us. As if he wouldn't be gulping in all sorts of information through his panoptics and scans anyway.

"Sure." Geoff glanced at me, the question evident in those

wide dark eyes. I shrugged, and made my fingers loosen on his arms.

He's taller. Had he really grown so much since we'd left the City, and I was just seeing it now after an absence? Or was it that he'd grown even since New Vega? The shape of his face seemed . . . different, too. Cheekbones higher, eyes a little smaller, his shoulders subtly changed. Broader, maybe. I began brushing the sand away from him as he shuddered and turned like a fourpad, my fingers testing the little bits of grit.

Below ground. Of course. It makes sense, that's why they didn't carry the shocktroopers out. All those stories. Fairytales and whispers, locked away in the dusty regions of pre-implementation memory, when the entire world was a warmbody's confusion instead of the clarity of implemented senses and intake feeds.

Just like the whispers about the Collective, those silver-eyed cyborgs without an agent's freedom of will. Some of the old stories called them *Borrg*, a word nobody knew the meaning of anymore.

I yanked him forward again, hugged him as hard as I could without hurting him. Still so fragile. Thin bones, an un-implemented skull.

But the shocktroopers were tough. If I can keep him alive long enough, will he be?

Alive and free. One was no good without the other. Or was that greedy of me? There's no use in dealing yourself into a game like this without it, though.

The silent weight of Sam's presence killed whatever I would have said. A facilitator might think he was seeing a weakness. A vulnerability. Something to exploit.

I wasn't about to confirm.

I finally was able to hold Geoff at arm's length, scanning him one more time just to make sure. "You could have been hurt. You could have been killed." My throat felt dry, even though there was no reason for the sensation. “I shouldn’t have left you.”

“They told me where to find you.” He was smiling, those pearly, perfect teeth gleaming as full dark descended. “And listen, they’re happy.”

Wolfsong rose again, a net of wild spunglass howling. What did they live on, out here? Probably the brothers and sisters of the small once-furry thing roasting on Sam’s fire, and if there were trees nearby there was bound to be bigger prey. “Did you go through the township? Did anyone see you?” The thought of him wandering right where I threw a bunch of hackbombs and brought down all sorts of attention made everything inside my skin feel like it was crawling into a different configuration.

“I traveled at night. Stayed away from the lights and the people, they’re not safe. The worms, well, they have tracks. Like roads. I followed those.” He shook his head, peered at me through his sand-stiffened hair. A slight movement, like he wanted to hug me, but I kept my arms straight and stiff. *Get him back into routine, he’s still just a kid. And Sam’s watching.*

“Good. Get some fresh clothes, the gear’s right there. Then it’s time to eat.”

He nodded, his face firming up. Darted another glance at Sam, who stared at the fire like it contained a Control directive.

“Don’t worry.” Softly, just barely audible, I said it as reassuringly as I could. “He’s on our side for now. The instant he isn’t, I’ll kill him again. And he’ll *stay* dead.”

“I can hear you,” Sam replied, mildly. Nothing on his face but the usual indifference, moonlight and fireglow working together to turn his skin a sickly shade mine probably matched. “Come on, kid, if we leave this any longer it’ll burn. Consider me your guardian angel, now.”

It was absurd . . . but it did make me feel better.

* * *

We rode abreast in the cold breathing unquiet of a desert night, fourpads chuffing a little among themselves, my own carefully between Sam's and Geoff's. A blurry inkstain on the horizon drew no closer no matter how we plodded, and Geoff swayed in the saddle. I decided I didn't want to question him any further until we were alone, and Sam didn't make any inquiries either.

Wise of him.

Geoff didn't ask where we were going, and neither did I. If Sam was leading us into a trap, well, it would hardly be worse than going back to Carsona. The locals there were about to get an influx of City types, and maybe it would do some of them a little good. Hard bitcoin would shower down, because even agents liked to eat.

So did other things. Maybe it would balance out the throat-ripping shocktroops.

After an hour of steady motion, I decided it was time. "Sam."

"Hm?" He kept his fourpad a little further away from mine than absolutely necessary. Also wise of him.

"The shocktroopers. Second-gens."

"Yeah." He scrubbed at his face with one stiff-bladed hand, as if weary. The faint amount of gold stubble rasping against his palm was intentional; probably habitual camouflage. "Helixes packed with anything they could scrape from your boy there."

I figured that much out, I'm not stupid. But if he wanted me to pull it out of him a piece at a time, I would. "Without nanos."

"They had to find the right recessives. Otherwise the packing slagged the experiments. The holy grail would be a breeding female, but they haven't figured that out yet."

"A breeding . . ." I glanced at Geoff, who looked supremely unconcerned. "Military applications, of course. But—"

"It's not just military." Sam took a deep breath. "It's evolution. Paxton was one of ours."

What? "An agent did this? I thought corporations wouldn't take implemented scientists." *At least, one carrying implants that weren't done in their own bays, under close supervision. Too easy for a competitor to sneak a tattletale into your processes and walk away with profitable secrets.*

Was it the light, or did he actually look pained? "Not Agency. One of *us*. Nikor's."

"Do you realize how ridiculous you sound?" I didn't even bother to keep the disgust out of my tone.

"Stranger than fiction," he muttered. "Do you ever wonder what the Agency's long-term plan is?"

I shrugged, knowing he'd catch the movement on panoptics. "Settled for just surviving, Sammy."

"One of these days I'll tell you my actual name."

"Don't care." I urged my fourpad closer to Geoff's. He swayed even more, a tired little boy, and it was a moment's work to lift him onto my saddle, settling him in front of me and grabbing his beast's lead-rope. My hands worked, paying out the lead so the shaggy beast wouldn't have to crowd. I could have just let it go, it would follow its furry friends, but better to be safe. "Shhh, kiddo. Rest."

"They said you were looking for me." Slow and sleepy, Geoff slumped against me. My autonomics finally settled, their subroutines nice and even. "Sorry, Abbymom."

"It's all right. Just glad you're safe." I didn't ask *who* told him that. Worms or wolves or whatever, it didn't matter at the moment, especially with another pair of ears around. I settled for arranging my reins again, breathing in the smell concentrated at the top of his head—dust and boy, and that faint astringency. Almost caustic, a familiar echo of gray rings and rotating teeth. "Rest."

"Shit." Sam's subvocal grumble disturbed his fourpad, but he shifted with the beast's motion. *"You really like this kid. Is that it?"*

"Long-term plan." I kept it barely audible. It really only took a moment or two to fit the pieces together, and even less than that to decide to ignore the rest of Sam's poking and prodding. "To profit from implementation as long as possible."

"Not quite." Sam sighed. "Imagine everyone on the planet, even the Waste-bred, with a basic level of implementation. Immortality for a price. That's been their game ever since the first nano breakthrough in '48. They're close to doing it, too. Clouds of nanos released, self-replicating, merging with human tissue and—"

"More fairytales. *Borrg.* Complete assimilation." I swiped at lank hair against my forehead. My thermal signature spread out, covering Geoff's. "Didn't they have holoshows about this?"

"Jess, we're going to get exactly nowhere if you keep that up."

"We're already nowhere." I pointed at the horizon. "Been nowhere since Egress. Don't mind it."

"How *did* you swing Egress? I can't figure it out."

A good agent never has just one card. I scanned the surroundings again. I was almost beginning to believe my kid was safe in front of me.

Sam sighed. "Anyway, they're close to completion, but there's an unexpected kink in the works. That kid. Paxton did something, and Nikor sent people to bring him *and* the kid in. Someone else jumped first. Paxton ended up dead, the kid got moved—"

"Doctor Pax," Geoff piped up, helpfully. "I remember him. He was nice. He wasn't like you, though. Cyborg."

I wished I could see Sam's expression. Would he wince at the word? We prefer *implemented.* The other, well, it means mindlessness.

The Collective. I wonder . . . Not enough data to tell.

"Do you remember what happened to him?" Sam, soft and cajoling.

I gave Geoff a warning squeeze, and he lapsed into silence, becoming boneless against me.

"The kid got moved," I supplied, "and you decided to send me after him, gambling that I'd feel like I was in over my head and come crying to you for some kind of help."

"The Agency sent a kill order through. It was lucky I was in rotation. I picked you because I thought . . . well, you were always my favorite, Jess."

"You keep saying that." I patted Geoff's arm, smoothed his hair. What was it like, for a kid, to hear someone say *kill order* just as if they were noting the weather, or the state of the fourpads? "So Nikor owns you." If I could believe in . . . what Geoff was, I could believe someone had dusted off the name of Nikor's Rebellion for their own purposes. Maybe there were even unicorns or holotrolls out there somewhere.

Or even Libera, that shining free city.

A long silence, swallowed up by the desert night, the fourpads breathing clouds of steam, their footfalls in a steady jog-jangle rhythm. I let Sam wait before I took the conversational bait. "What does your fairytale want with my kid?"

"We still don't know how Paxton did it. If we can decode him, even if the Agency goes ahead with Omega we'll have recourse. Kid rejects nanos wholesale, and there's got to be a way to replicate it, pack the helixes with his capabilities. Imagine, no more cancer, no more slag mutations, no more of the Agency having a lock on living and breathing in-City. You think the corporations own everything? Didn't you get the memo about who owns *them*?"

My arms tightened fractionally. *Not sure I ever cared to follow the whole stinking trail that far.* There never appeared to be any point.

Sam continued. "The only reason that kid's still alive is because CoreTech provided cover for what Pax was doing. Agency used Niful as catspaw to nab him, since Operations wanted to study him before they liquidated; Control found out and sent through the kill order. *You* were a bare twenty minutes ahead of a capture team from Control's research side. Turf wars, you have no idea about the sodding turf wars." A shake of his pale head. "The only place you're going to be safe now is—"

"Spare me." I smoothed Geoff's hair again, stroking away sand and a thin crusting reflexive chemtesting gave me that familiar profile on. Something damp had smeared the grit against the strands, then dried. *Look at those lovely peptides.* "Paxton was either from out-City or he had Egress license. Which was it?"

"He had black-card research clearance." Did dear old Sammy sound surprised? "Full Egress whenever he . . . why?"

Huh. "Where are you headed?"

"Last communication told me to head into the Vines. We'll be picked up."

Not sure I want to be "picked up." I wasn't sure of a whole lot in this current situaion. But I let it go, for one very basic reason.

It's always good to have a little cannon fodder around.

Of course even a desert would have a suburb full of greenery. Which might make the sand-glare the Ring, with its own stacked-stone skyscrapers and aristocracy. Except in-City, royalty is never that threadbare.

Or are they? Maybe the true aristocracy rumbles under the sand, just like it moves invisibly through a City's human tides. A corporation gets to a certain size, and it stops behaving like a "group" and starts being a crowd—an organism with a mind of its own. A sort of basement sentience fills its tentacles, and there's no going back. Despite Sam's hints, I thought it goddamn likely it was that foggy artificial intelligence that made all the moves, and the rest of us just scrabbled to keep up.

The only way out was just what Geoff and I had done—opt into the wilderness. If everyone else did, the makers and breakers in their offices would have nothing left. *That* was something for them to fear, and the large, terrible tumors we called corporations would react with furious activity to every vanishing prospect of such a demise.

"I've seen maps." Sam frowned at the steaming green wall at the edge of the sand. "But . . . ugh."

A carpet of already-wilting wildflowers, briefly blossoming after the rains, unraveled a discreet distance from a steep slope. Their starry little faces full of cheerful color stared, surprised, at the sun that would end their small freedom soon enough.

Looking up from their dying beauty, the first thing you noticed was a mist, exhaling in loops and fringes from a mass of inchoate, sinuous shapes.

The Vines. They don't move, they only seem to when the wind ruffles the thready masses at the tops of their snakelike stalks. Brown creepers loop crazily between them, encasing the trunks in a web like a spinwool sweater—cut one knot, and the entire thing unravels. Further up the slope the . . . trees, I guess you had to call them, started to grow taller. The jagged demarcation was the same in either direction—wilting flowers petering out, a narrow strip of darker sand, probably mixed with a stratum underneath, thin-fingering vines clawing at the beginnings of soil. Then the shrubs, growing mathematically taller as they receded from the killing heat of the desert pan.

A shy, secretive breeze slid past us, the desert breathing into the Vines. I sniffed deeply, testing.

That much greenery meant moisture. The fourpads snorted, a little unhappily, so I swung down from the saddle. I toed the dark sand and realized the creepers were secreting a chemical cocktail to keep any desert vegetation a comfortable distance away. Thick drops of clear moisture collect on the undersides of the fingering vines, and it soaked into the sand to prepare for the greenery to spread itself.

I glanced up at Geoff, who looked a little sallow in the moonlight. The greenery would mean more mammals, maybe even some large ones to whet his thirst. So far we hadn't had to sacrifice a fourpad . . . but it was close.

I suppressed a sigh. Remounted with a creak, and eyed Sam. He wasn't keeping a tight lid on his autonomics, *or* on his mouth. Maybe he thought I'd trust him if he chattered, or if I could hear his buffered pulse loud and clear.

In any case, he said there was a township a few days into the Vines. Once we got there, he would ping for pickup, whether by his fairytale or by the Agency didn't matter. Since Carsona would be crawling with those hunting Geoff, all I had to do slip us both free of Sam at the right time, and let them chase their tails and his, too.

My handler probably mistook my look for interest, or for needing direction. "There should be a path a little north of here."

I nodded. Geoff's face was a white dish. He asked no questions. I didn't know whether to be happy about that.

I pointed my fourpad north, and Geoff's followed.

Two hours later, we plunged into the night under the Vines, lit only by faint fungal phosphorescence. The fourpads didn't like it, and neither did I.

We went anyway.

CHAPTER NINE

I THINK SHE'S SERIOUS

During the day, the canopy turned everything below into aqueous green shimmer that didn't raise blistering welts on Geoff's skin. He avoided the faint specks and columns of unfiltered sunshine, but I caught him holding his hands out in the green glow more than once, marveling at the shadows rippling.

There was enough in the light to capture a bit of solar, and an agent can live even on poisonous greenery if she has to. It wasn't necessary, the solar was enough. The edge of the Vines is scattered with small townships, a necklace of stragglers living in moss-covered shacks—but we avoided those.

Steam and constant dripping from the canopy made it humid as a Bonnell tank, and the condensation on every surface encouraged thin traceries of green scum to spread in filigreed waves. Before long, anything you didn't scrub or waterproof turned slimy, then almost-dry as the moss thickened, its deep restful green hiding slightly caustic root-drippings. Slow creatures hung from the canopy, their fur festooned with matted colonies of plant and insect matter; the avians had bright, thickly oiled feathers and deafening screeches. The slow hanging carpets—Sam called them *pilosas*—carried a slew of noisome toxins in their flesh, which probably explained why they hadn't been hunted out of existence.

There were other things, though. Mammals both small and large, reptiles quick and slow, and the warmbodies eking out whatever living they could out here.

The first few townships were corporate; we faded back into the greenery and bypassed them after a battery of cautious scans. No linkups, though they all had steadily-pinging drop beacons. Safe below the canopy, Sam and I heard the thrumming of thopters and the swish of silver-needle droppers and eyes.

The amount of silver-needles bothered me, until I realized it would only take one bandit with a cobbled-together stat-cannon—or even a plasma cannon stolen from somewhere—to bring down most thopters the Cities could send out. Droppers and eyes could keep the area around a township clear, and lock onto any statbolt signature big enough to drop a thopter while the weapon was powering up. Transports are too big to bring down with just one stat-cannon, large enough to have their own defense systems too.

At least there was no shortage of fluids for my kid.

The first was a wild porcine—large enough to be awkward, but breaking most of its ribs took most of the fight out of it. Geoff drank quickly, flushing as I watched, his throat moving as I held the bulky thing up by its hind legs against a tree-trunk as large around as a slagshack. Sam watched, his face the same expressionless mask it had been in-City, which was a relief.

It took a while, but Geoff finished like a good little boy and stepped back, wiping at his mouth. A hot sheen over his dark gaze, and it wasn't just imagination or wishful thinking.

He *was* taller. His face was changing, settling against the bones differently. Instead of the pale, scrawny eight-ish kid he'd been in-City, he looked like a twelve-year-old runner. Lean and quick, just on the edge of adolescence, a shadow of adult knowledge far back in his dark gaze. His hair was no longer City-lank or sand-stiffened, but a halo of dark, springy waves. The scar on his chin flushed, a ribbon of crimson, and he blinked a couple times, his cheeks pooching a little as if it was going to come back up.

"You all right?" I held the dead bulk of the porcine by its cracking back legs. There is a definite change in a body when life is finally gone. The thing's labored breathing had shuddered to a stop some time ago, and the rest of nerve-death quivered through it in decreasing waves.

"Tastes . . ." He shook his head a little. "Spicy, almost. Wild. They fight, you know. All the big animals do."

"Yeah." I braced myself, heaved at the inert bulk; it rolled down a slight slope alive with those tangled creepers and knobby dark roots. More bones snapped as it rolled. We could have eaten some of it, but it wasn't worth the effort of carrying around. Not while there was solar coming through the treetops. "Living means fighting."

"Always?" Wiping at his mouth again, as if the blood burned.

"Not always." How could I explain that when you couldn't fight, you had to run? Or that there might be people somewhere who didn't betray you, but they were few and far between? Maybe he already knew. "But close enough."

He swayed forward, like he did after every large feeding, and I held him. Sam kept watching, that blank green-tinted mask. He could have been a statue left to rot here in the Vines, his hair fading into greening brass instead of wheat, his hands loose and easy, the fourpads behind him rustling nervously in the foliage. They seemed to be able to graze on the smaller bushes just fine, and I was almost certain there were herds of them—or something similar—passing through the jumble at night. Scat and scrapes against the tough creeper-roots, certainly herbivore, not hooved like the porcines or scythe-clawed like the fluid, tree-climbing felines.

Maybe next time I should catch him one of those. I breathed into his hair, he hugged me as hard as his frail little arms could.

Sam still stared. I stared back, sap and condensation turning my dark hair to matted strings hanging over my eyes, down to my chin. *Go ahead. Start chattering. Tell me we'll make contact soon. Act like you're not lost.*

Insects buzzed and ticked. The birds, used to us by now, had resumed their deafening chorus. Cataloging all the species would be enough to keep even an agent busy for years. As it was, I had a record going constantly. All that data might be good for something later.

You never know.

"I don't like it." Geoff's breath was a hot spot in the middle of my soaked shirt. "Why can't we have a house?"

Like that's any insurance. But that wasn't anything to tell a kid. "We do have one." I stroked his hair. The moss slid right off the coarse strands, easily shed. "It's the entire world, kiddo. You and me, under the sky."

"You and me," he repeated. At least he didn't sound doubtful about that. "I used to watch the holos and think about being, you know. One of them."

"That's what holos are supposed to do." I didn't want to let him go, but he wriggled a bit. So I released him, brushed away moss, straightened the sleeves of his Static Rebe T-shirt—now stained with sap, the spincotton developing pinpoint holes as it rotted under the constant high humidity. "Make you want something different than what you've got."

"Isn't that good?" The pooching in his cheeks went away, his color smoothed out. With his eyes half-lidded he was a sleepy kid again. "*He* says there's a rebellion. That means wanting what you haven't got, right?"

"It can." I turned back to the patiently waiting fourpads, one of them chewing a mouthful of cud and fresh greens with an abstract expression. Their tough, clawed feet adapted well to the damp, and they were looking glossy and sleek. "More often, it just means someone else wants to be on top of the pyramid, and that's all."

"Cynic." Sam offered me the reins. "There are altruists in the world, Jess."

"Yeah. They usually die first." I watched Geoff swing himself up in the saddle. "Don't facilitators study history?"

"Extensively." He waited until I was in the saddle before climbing aboard his own fourpad. "We're close now. Shouldn't be more than another couple days."

"So you *do* have a destination."

"Always." There was no tinge of untruth to the word, but of course that was another implemented capability.

Good to know. "And?"

"We're going to Libera."

Wonderful. Why didn't you say so? We'll fly on multicolored thopters and eat all the soya cream and not get sick. I didn't even bother to ask. It would probably end up being another fairytale.

Except by now, I was uncomfortably certain Sam was telling the unvarnished truth.

The light drained away sharply, darkness falling like a City district during shutoff. None of the desert's vibrant dusk, none of the furious glory of red and gold to the west. I didn't think I'd miss it . . . but I did. I even missed the rumblegrumble of worms in the distance, the desiccation of the oven-hot wind, and the sense that you could see trouble coming a long distance away.

False comfort, maybe, but better than nothing.

More than once—as Sam started a recalcitrant fire in the evening, coaxing the spatters of amber sap into burning enough to dry out vines and other small bits of combustible matter—I was startled into a grim amusement. Two agents carrying implementation worth tidy piles of bitcoin hard or flex, a kid worth everything to several corporations, an outlay of resources from the Agency that rivaled the perpetual hunting-down of rogue elements to erase, and here we were, huddled around a miserable fire for an hour or so before scattering to sleep in the treetops. At least, I slept high up. Geoff, well . . .

It's quiet, he told me softly. *It's nice and dark and soft. You should try it.*

Seeing him sink through the roots, the earth opening to receive his slight body, everything scrabbling over the top to seamlessly hide him, even the leafmulch and vines thick around as my legs—now I knew exactly how the shocktroopers had hidden. I couldn't figure out if I should call it focused telekinesis or just . . . magic. Either was equally likely, and equally frustrating for an agent.

It almost made me wish I'd stayed in Carsona to witness the tangle when everyone and their clone descended to find Geoff and instead stumbled across CoreTech's free-range second-gens. They were probably *still* sorting out the mess. With the security force depleted, it would look like someone had deliberately hit a corporate town to provoke a response. My intentionally clumsy hacking, tripping alarms everywhere, would only muddy the waters.

It hadn't all been ham-fisted. For instance, I'd managed to slide my way into a restricted CapTech section, figuring that a mining corp would have maps of the areas surrounding not only its own satellite townships, but also its competitors'. And lo, I had hit what they used to call paydirt, there and in a couple other corporations. It didn't matter so much that I had burned a couple of carefully-nurtured access dumps—the whole point of the hacking was to point fingers at the Agency where possible, and at competitors for every single corp whose data I went tripping through.

As a result, I knew we were about a day and a half away from a suspiciously blank part of every map I could have cracked my way into even with Agency clearance.

And that was interesting.

"Hey, kid." Sam had taken to beaming at Geoff, a development I watched narrowly but let take its course. "Want to help me nurse this?"

Geoff glanced at me for approval, and I shrugged.

"The sap burns," he said finally, settling just out of Sam's reach.

Smart kid.

"Resinous. Smells good when goes, too. Can I ask you something?"

I busied myself with the gear. Facilitators, always poking and prying.

"I suppose." Geoff, laconic as a liquidator.

"Do you like her?" A sudden movement, pointing at me. Probably to gauge whether the kid would flinch.

He didn't, just gave Sam a level look, tossing a thin stick into the wan flames. It sent up a thin ribbon of white smoke, and Geoff's flushed mouth was now a subtle curve.

"She's my mom." Quietly, as if daring the other agent to disagree.

"So that's a yes, huh? She takes care of you, kisses you goodnight, all that happy holo stuff. Right?"

"Yeah." Geoff's gaze slid away, towards the fire. "You're wondering if this will burn me."

"There's legends."

"I know." Now Geoff even sounded amused. "You could try while I was sleeping. Or maybe not."

"You think she'd stop me?"

What the hell did Sam think he was doing? The strings inside me tightened, tightened a little more. The packs were going to rot right through and split unless I could find a better waterproofing than the resin dripping from the treetops. It was amazing the whole Vines didn't go up like a candle, but so much moisture in the air precluded ignition. Where did it all come from? The tree-things breathed vapor daily, maybe that was it. The Vines made its own weather.

Geoff regarded him levelly. "She'd kill you again. Even though she likes you."

I don't like him. He's just useful, and until I have a better idea, it's good to have a little cannon fodder. Still, it was . . . nice, maybe? To have a piece of the familiar around.

Familiar is dangerous. It slows you down, dulls a sharp blade. I smeared more resin on the bottom of the packs, ignoring the tingle along my skin as the nanos moved to neutralize essential oils and various thought-provoking compounds in it. Geoff didn't seem to mind the stuff, just wiping it off his skin.

Sam continued. "Maybe she likes both of us. Maybe she's just keeping you alive to sell you. Ever think of that?"

Maybe a facilitator just couldn't see anything good without wanting to piss all over it. Or maybe he thought driving a wedge between me and the kid would serve him later on. Who knew?

I can tell you what Sam didn't expect, though.

Geoff froze for a long moment, the crackling of flames finally taking hold on the damp wood. Later, replaying the event, I would decide that the fire had leapt a bit, then flattened in front of Geoff before he moved.

"You take that back!" the kid yelled, launching himself across the campfire.

He hit Sam squarely, and actually knocked the facilitator over backward. I dropped the saddlepack, coiled myself, and blurred across the intervening space, but not before a wild flail of arms and legs windmilling around had managed to connect a few times.

Normally a warmbody wouldn't be able to even *touch* an agent. But by the time I pulled Geoff away, his teeth champing together with heavy sounds like the thumping of a railgun a City district away, the scar on his chin separating to give the jaw more room to morph and his limbs blurring in ways no warmbody's should, Sam was actually *bleeding*.

"Enough." I hauled Geoff back, and it took more force than I liked. They were both deadly silent, and I almost tossed the kid into a tree just to get him *away* in case this had given Sam the opening he wanted all along.

Instead, the facilitator stayed down, limbs splayed crookedly, his pale gaze distant as he watched me pin Geoff's wildly moving arms and drag him back. The contusions on Sam's cheeks vanished swiftly, nanos doing their duty by their host. A few shallow slices sealed themselves away, the silver motes in the black fluid—sunlight had retreated, and blood always looks black at night—burrowing back in through the skin once they'd finished repair work.

I held Geoff until he went limp, his breath coming in harsh gasps. "You take that *back*!" he screamed, and if nobody knew we were in the forest, that would probably change in the next few minutes, because the dusk cacophony stilled. A bubble of silence expanded in the Vines, like those first few hushed moments we had slipped through a tangle of those heavy, rough-skinned tentacles and found ourselves in the mist.

"Let him go." Sam didn't move. He just lay there, a discarded toy, probably grinning on the inside because he'd provoked a huge response. "Let's see if he really means it."

That spurred Geoff to fresh motion, but my arms tightened. He was strong.

Too strong. *Agent*-strong.

What is this kid going to grow up into? A shocktrooper, maybe, snarling and blurring through space as he ripped the throats out of fragile little warmbodies? They hadn't just taken the blood.

No, they'd *bathed* in it.

"That is *enough*." My tone cut through Geoff's struggles, and he went limp. The silence thickened, like a respite tank or the moment on a rooftop before the firing starts, just after you realize someone's anticipated the route you thought was safe. "He's a *facilitator*, Geoff. That means he wants to find out what's inside your head so he can make you do what he wants. Stop making it easy for him."

"I think she's serious," Sam piped up.

"Shut up." I didn't bother looking at him. "It's just like at the institute, kid. Watching you in that fishbowl, waiting for a reaction. Don't give him one."

"You gonna teach him to clamp his autonomics, Jess? A nice happy family, just you and a bloodsucking experiment? How long is it going to be before you can't control him and he starts eating slaggers whole?"

Geoff tensed. I didn't move. His springy hair tickled my nose. His pulse was fluttering wings, the little flicking jewel-toned avians whose sharp beaks probed the vibrant, scentless flowers halfway up the trunks where the sunlight intensified. Moving so fast they blurred, you never saw them perching.

My grip gentled. I stroked Geoff's hair with my chin, once, twice.

"Nikor can teach him what he is. How to control himself." Sam's tongue flicked over his lips, and I found myself wishing the sap would override his nanos and poison the fuck out of him. "Where he came from. Who he—"

"Keep going." I didn't have to work to sound tired and unwelcoming. "Go ahead."

That shut him up. Geoff's pulse smoothed out, dropped. His breathing still came jagged and harsh, but after a few moments I couldn't hear his heartbeat at all.

Great. I nodded, as if he'd done something expected. "Good job, sweetheart." My arms eased even more. If he went for Sam again, I wasn't going to restrain him. "Put a little more on the fire, we don't want it to go out."

He swallowed, audibly. Sam didn't move, watching with bright avid interest. I ignored it, but this shifted the entire dynamic a bit.

There's only so much you can allow cannon fodder.

"Jess." Sam, subvocalizing. *"He's not your kid."*

The fuck he's not, I thought, but I let it go. That seemed to finish up Sam's attempt at pushing Geoff to show more of whatever interesting new talents he was developing, and while my kid stared hotly at the facilitator when he eventually hauled himself up and brushed himself off, there was no more sparring.

The next evening, we rode into what Sam called "Libera."

"Smith?" Sam shook his head. The moss clinging to the strands made them move life Geoff's. "All this time? Sam *Smith*?"

"Like I said. Alliterative." My fourpad, still kept carefully between theirs as we rode single-file, snorted a counterpoint to the word.

"But *why*?" Did he actually sound piqued?

If so, I was happy about it.

"Names are important." I stretched my back a little, tightening a muscular algorithm. Damn beasts would wreck a warmbody riding them, why were they so common out here? "Until they're not."

"That why the kid calls you Abby?"

Of course he had to ask. "No." I squinted at the canopy overhead. Thinning out a bit, and there was no doubt that we were getting close to civilization—or what passed for it out here. That blank space on the map.

There were other blank spaces on the continent, too. It was enough to make a girl think. I knew the world was round, and I knew there were other landmasses out there.

The maps that would show me those either didn't exist, or were under heavily encrypted lock and key . . . or they didn't matter. It was an article of faith that the Gene Wars had rendered much of the planet uninhabitable, at least by warmbodies. Spores in the air, bioweapons lurking in the soil, mutations drifting and curdling everywhere, just waiting to creep into your own body and start causing trouble.

It had also been an article of faith that the Waste would kill you as soon as you stepped outside City walls, and if it didn't the radiation or the cannibals would. The corporation townships were supposed to be only for criminals and rejects, City castoffs who worked hard and died young. Yet there were warmbodies all over the place who had never seen the inside of a City, eking out a living. Even the cannibals had a rough approximation of societal rules, and traded for items they couldn't make, scavenge, or raid.

It had never made sense to me in-City, but I'd been too busy thinking about other things. Now, outside, it still didn't make any sense, but I had to figure it out posthaste.

Somewhere, there had to be a hidden corner where someone wouldn't be hunting down this kid. I just had to find it.

Of course, Sam would ask me *why*. Didn't matter.

"You've noticed he's growing." Sam peered past me as Geoff's fourpad picked its delicate way along the approximation of a path behind mine. "And he's showing signs."

I stared past the tuft of hair atop my fourpad's bobbing head. *Signs of what?* A useless question.

I slept below . . . they sing, you know.

What else would he end up being able to do? He was already much stronger than a warmbody should be, and faster, too. As fast as those second-gens?

Would he heal like them?

If the shield of green above grew patchier, we would have to wait until full night to travel. The Vines took its regular evening breath, the feathery canopy rustling, mist and steam curling between trunks and trashwood. The tree-things here were tall but relatively spindly, and the choking underbrush told me this part had been clearcut not too long ago as such things went. Added to that, the tangle of animal paths and guesswork we'd been following had turned into a reasonably well-traveled track, and there was ionization drawing nearer and nearer. Very little in the way of thopter or needle sounds overhead, and I didn't hear a pinging for drops.

Of course, in a blank spot . . .

What the hell is that?

A shimmer crackled to life between the trunks and hanging vines. It wasn't stat, it wasn't plasma, it wasn't lectric.

Geoff pulled his fourpad to a halt, because I'd done the same. "Mom?"

"You see that?" I beckoned a little, and his fourpad stepped back. By this time, Geoff only needed to give the beast a slight indication of which direction to step and it obeyed willingly, its hair festooned with moss that didn't seem to bother it.

"Not exactly. Feel it, though." Geoff's eyes were round, gleaming in the failing dusk. "Something's wrong."

"Nope." Sam's teeth showed, a wide white smile. "That's just Libera. There's geothermals all through the Vines, and this one's large enough to power a Trapp core and turbines. You're looking at a Trapp field."

I had to ping a blue-section scan on the shimmer in front of me, and it returned a spiky energy signature I never thought I'd ever see in person. "Huh."

"Is it safe?" Geoff made an inquiring movement with his dark, bushy head. "I don't feel good. Something's wrong."

"I don't feel good either." I eyed Sam. "When were you going to share this news?"

"Couldn't be sure we'd all get here." His tone plainly shouted *especially in one piece*. "And . . ."

"And?"

"And, um, I'm not supposed to have brought you this way." He shifted uncomfortably in the saddle. "I was *supposed* to take you to a pickup point west, out in the *tepuis*. Transport was supposed to be waiting. But it's the damndest thing, Jess. I can't raise my contact even through emergency methods. And it feels hinky. Remember TakedaCorp and the shitfest that turned into?"

It's not like I can forget. My pulse tried to speed up, a subroutine clamped down. The shimmer in the air taunted me. The TakedaCorp pressure had gone sideways in a big way. I knew what it was like to be parted out and dropped into corrosive sludge.

And after all, it had been Sam who'd fished me out. Dealing with the psych responses after your first dismemberment is unpleasant, to say the least.

Of course, this could be a facilitator's game. I could be expected to feel some loyalty, right? That's what he wanted.

"I didn't want you to worry." He touched his heels to his fourpad's sides, and the beast moved forward. They slid through the shimmerfield with a brief fluorescing, man and fourpad limned like digital echoes.

I exhaled sharply, and Geoff watched me. Waiting for direction.

Our supplies were low. I could turn the fourpads loose and carry Geoff, swinging from tree to tree. Shimmy up into the canopy to get a solar charge while he slept safely below during the day. He could live off the porcines here handily.

They are closely related to humans, you know.

If we did that, Sam wouldn't be far behind.

"Abbymom?" Tentative, Geoff kneeing his fourpad closer. "He could be telling the truth."

"How do you know?" I shook my head. It was useless to start questioning now. "We might as well go on in."

Geoff kneed his fourpad forward, and I was about to follow, when the silence bloomed all around me and every instinctive hackle on me bristled.

That was when they hit me, knocking me right through the shimmer.

The second-gens could live on the bigger mammals as well. And if Geoff could find me, of course his cousins could, too.

CHAPTER TEN

NON-ALLIANCE

The fourpad exploded, chunks of meat flying and a starburst of hot blood. It died silently, the beast with the tufted swirl on his head, and oddly enough, that was I thought about as I tumbled free of the statrifle blast.

I liked him, dammit.

I was buffered. The fourpad wasn't.

I tumbled through the Trapp field just before it turned crystalline-solid, reacting to the statblast. That's the great thing about them—if you have the power to waste, that type of field will immediately react to stat, projectile fire, and plasma. Of course, anyone who throws plasma at a Trapp field has to be prepared for the plas to yank on all available energy in its vicinity and rebound on the idiot who fired it. A nice bonus, but again, you had to have the power to burn. If you could link one of them to a solar complex big enough you could have your own impregnable enclave—and you'd need it full of cheap labor, too, just to keep the solarcatchers polished.

Hit with a *crunch*, reinforced bones bending instead of snapping, tumbling over roots and tile-hard brown-husked vines. Now that I was through the shimmer, intake feeds and scans crackled into life, a breaker of hideous feedback before I adjusted, already scrambling with my feet underneath me. Channels both encrypted and non, high chatter and a massive thrumming, ionization and statrepeller fields contributing their own special burning tinge to air I'd grown used to smelling only sap and animals in.

Geoff screamed, a high piercing cry. Two of the second-gens had gotten through before the shimmer hardened, and the others—how many, couldn't tell, had they picked up their fourth member? Could they survive a probe through the chest cavity? In any case, they would be through as soon as the Trapp field cycled back down. The fourpads bolted, their claw-pad feet throwing up dirt and glistening chunks of vines, furrowing deep pale scars in the earth as they decided anywhere was better than here.

I didn't blame them.

Sam blurred, tumbled free of his fourpad and rolling. Geoff still clutched the reins of his own fear-maddened beast, and his curly head bobbed as he held on for dear life with his knees, hunching down and curling his fingers in a handful of mane as well.

I almost, *almost* streaked after him. It would be simple to catch the fourpads, and Sam's held all his gear. The plasma cannon was in Geoff's pack, broken apart for easier transport—at least we didn't have to worry about it getting crushed and its core reacting with the Trapp field.

It would take them a little while to deal with Sam. That was long enough for both Geoff and me to get some distance.

A crackle, another sizzle, and a thump. I whirled, moss flying from my hair. I was already in the air, committed to my leap, before I thought about what I was doing. Simple, really—Sam would slow them down, but not enough.

He wasn't a liquidator.

The blond had a lectricshiv, shoved deep in Sam's belly. My handler twitched a kick, a knee breaking with a greenstick crack, and the other second-gen—the one with bones in his hair, clacking as he moved—had Sam's arms pinned. The tactic was pretty clear: tear him in half.

It wasn't anything Sam wouldn't recover from, unless they put his halves on either side of the Trapp barrier. But still. It was the *principle* of the thing.

Using principles to justify what we want now, agent? That's a bad sign.

A snap-kick as I landed, throwing the bone-haired monstrosity into the barrier. The shimmering squeal-crackled and the second-gen howled, his face twisted up into purple pleats and valleys, those teeth gleaming as they snapped together with a heavy, sickeningly familiar sound.

The blond launched himself at me, his navy shocktrooper gear sadly mangled both from combat and the rot of the Vines. They must have been following us for a while, and Geoff's immunity to the moss and resinous drippings might not be completely shared.

I had no knife but I was ready, and more than ready, I had them calculated. They were fast, yes. Brutal, yes. Very durable, too.

But they were *stupid*.

Dropping, my foot flickering up to sink into the blond's abdomen and help him on his merry way, with a little twist at the end to hopefully toss him near the curvature of the shimmerfield. Which squealed afresh—had some idiot on the other side hit it with another stat jolt? It would keep this section of the field locked down, impermeable.

Amateurs. Knees pulled in, a reverse somersault, uncoiling and touching down on a tangle of vines, one of my boots almost disintegrating from rot and stress. Didn't matter, I was already in the air again as the bone-haired no-longer-warmbody—what the hell did you call these things, anyway, other than terms from other fairytales and old moldering pre-War legends? In any case, he slid down the inside of the shimmerfield, his clothes smoke-steaming. Sam was already on his feet again, tearing the lectricshiv free of his belly with one contemptuous, fluid motion, spinning it to hold reversed along his forearm. Nanos swarmed, silver crawling among the blood and a grayish looping dangle of intestine sucking itself back in, and I caught a long hank of bone-studded hair. Landed, set my heels and *yanked*, but the second-gen had his wits about him and just dropped, twisting fluidly to strike at my belly. The punch might have gone right through me, but you could tell he was used to tearing apart warmbodies. No real challenge, no reason for him to hone his enhanced strength. Battering ram only works if your power is unmatched.

Hand blurring down, caught his wrist, reflexes loosening my left knee and using the power of his strike to pull him *past*, spinning him with the force he so helpfully provided.

A childhood spent dodging other runners and a career outthinking other agents and heavily implemented warmbodies with more than two brain cells to rub together was great practice for this. I broke his neck again, arms closing around his shoulders in a hug, my knees in his back, and from there it was only a fractional application of force to change direction just a touch, slinging myself down and around like a stat-crawling wreckball on a crane for slum renewal, and his spine gave way with a defeated *snap*.

I wasn't finished yet. Oh no. I heard another howl—the blond, but I couldn't worry about Sam just yet. If he kept the other one occupied for a few seconds I could finish this.

Warmbody flesh, even enhanced with whatever they'd tinkered with to make Geoff and these awful cousins of his, parts so easily. I just had to hook my fingers and drag, and viscera spilled wetly out. That was just to keep him down, though, because my other hand curled around his nape. For a moment we were nose to nose, his rank breath spilling past my parted lips, those teeth snapping fruitlessly—he got a mouthful of my hair and sheared it, a whole moss-laden chunk—while my hand cramped closed, a vise whose two prongs found the edge between the cervicals and the diagonal of the sternocleidomastoids, puncturing ruthlessly and diving between nerve cables, I had a grip on the cervical spine itself and *hauled*, bone splintering and puncturing my own skin.

Didn't matter. *Hauled* again, finding just the right rotation to work the cable free without snapping it, and the cry that burst out of me when I tore the top half of the motherfucker's spine free, whipping it behind me with a spatter of blood, trailing nerve-strings, and flying moss, was another echo from the beginning of warmbody history.

We don't ever change biology. We just build on *top* of it, like Nature folding a whole new brain around a lizard-stem.

I was on my feet again, spinning as my naked heel slipped, and I saw Sam in a loose easy crouch, wrenching back the blond's head as he sawed at the neck with the lectricshiv. Its blade spat and hissed, glowing blue-white and cauterizing. With a final crack and a heave, he wrenched the head free, and tossed it aside. Nerve-death took over, the body bucking and kicking, and gouts of blood cooked on the lectricshiv's blade and the Trapp field, smoke-steaming and sending up a heavy copper reek.

Look at that. Wonder if that'll really kill them.

Sam's face was a pale dish, spattered with blood. His shirt flapped as he moved, blurring, and the *crack* of him ripping the second-gen's arm from its socket was shortly followed by another. More gushing and welling, splatting heavily. How much blood did they hold?

Just like the tiny pinprick insects who buried their head in your skin and tried to suck. The nanos made me impervious, and Geoff simply brushed them off. Like the sap, and the clouds of midges.

Sam glanced at me. A silent snarl, lips pulled back from gleaming implemented teeth, and it was the first time, in years of meeting him in anonymous restaurants and back alleys and the weeks of out-City traveling, that I actually saw *past the screen of his job and into the man.*

I wasn't always a facilitator, Jess.

It had to be true.

The moment passed. He tossed the other arm aside, carelessly, and stood. A quick stamp, ribs snapping like branches, slivers of bone flying. He snapped a look at the Trapp field, beginning to lose its crystalline hardness. "Not a lot of time."

"They were going to tear you in half."

"They intended to try. Why did you stop them?"

Can you guess? "Maybe I just want to kill you myself."

"Thanks. I think."

"Mom!" Geoff's piping cry brought me around again. He'd managed to get the fourpads under control. "There's more of them!"

Sam's hand clamped around my arm. "Get into Libera. Hide, but don't go down below. I'll deal with them." I almost twitched away, but he jerked on my arm again, with more-than-warmbody strength. "Okay?"

I hesitated. Flickers of movement past him, outside the shimmerfield. "There's at least a half-dozen. You're not implemented for this."

He shrugged, the door of his face slamming shut. Just like a facilitator. "Jess. *Go*."

The fourpads sidled and made their nervous noises when I arrived in a blur next to them. I swung up on Sam's, and Geoff, deathly pale, stared over his shoulder. "I can hear them," he whispered. "They don't want *us*. They want *him*."

"They're going to get their wish," I muttered, my knees clamping home as Sam's cantankerous fourpad decided he might as well try to take charge of the situation. He'd chosen a beast just like him, the bastard. "Come on."

"We can't just—" Geoff swallowed the rest of whatever he planned on saying when I glanced at him. Behind us, the Trapp field hummed, its resonance losing the sharp clarity of solidity.

"Come on." I kneed the fourpad forward, and Geoff's followed. They picked up into a shattering, ungainly jog, and I heard more crackling and ripping sounds behind us.

We moved faster.

This Libera—probably Sam's little joke, to call it that—was built *around* the trees, and *up* their rough-fiber towers. The Trapp generators were mostly underground, but their humped backs rose almost to the canopy, the couplings atop them sending up a column of faint shimmer that reached a ceiling defined by Martell's Equations and umbrella'd out and down. The result was a rough circle, its surface area a bit larger than the average township—but they used every tree-thing's trunk and the network of thick vines to hold sheets of processed resin and build *upwards*, making almost-translucent walls. The ceilings and floors were tinted to make them darker, and detritus from outside the Vines had made its way even here. Pressboard, plasilca fragments, gutted transport hulls cradled in tree-things that had probably been planted right after the Wars.

Comchatter. The faint thunderous sound of conversation, echoes bouncing through the trees. The resin walls and windows glowed amber—lectric was free here, another benefit of the Trapp generators. There was little in the way of trash—maybe, I thought, everything was used or tossed into the generators' cores. The geothermals provided energy and to spare, but it was like the nanos—why make what you depended on for survival work harder than it absolutely had to?

There were no defenses. No statcannons, not even a guard perimeter. Geoff and I plunged into a labyrinth of passages on the outskirts, and a fine mist drifted down from sprayers far overhead. My vision blurred slightly before the nanos analyzed and blocked it. *Interesting. Chem signature there . . . they make this from the resin too. No wonder they don't need defenses. A few minutes of this and any warmbody will be too happy-dappy to fight.*

"It smells funny." Geoff's nose squinched up. "Wet. Nasty."

"Mild narcotic." A shudder ran through me as the nanos finished dispelling it and began manufacturing blockers. "Do you feel sleepy?"

He shook his head. "It just smells weird." But he yawned, hugely. A tired child, the tips of his sharp white teeth flashing once. "You think they'll kill him?"

"Maybe." *And I won't be there to put him back together.* The commchatter kept going, and I squinted. Crowd noises, but I saw nobody. My scans came back negative, too. The confusing haze from the resinous windows, refracting and filtering scans in weird fractals, didn't help.

"I don't . . ." Geoff swayed. I put out a hand to brace him. "Huh. Funny."

Fuck. This was all wrong. There was crowd-sound, and commchatter, but my scans didn't show a blessed thing. The lack of litter began to bother me even more. Not so much as a wrapper or a dropped spanner to mar the vine-tangled forest floor. Moss hung in great sheets, and the further we penetrated the tangle, the more my unease sharpened.

It was almost a relief to come around a corner, Geoff straightening and shaking off the narcotic haze, and see a human shape.

Except it wasn't. It was an agent, all in black, with a black wide-brimmed hat straight out of Cris Zifter holos. Male, a little taller than Sam, wide shoulders and my scans pinging on weird valleys and mountains in his nanoprofile. The tingle of being scanned in return slid over my skin, and my fourpad pushed forward, Geoff halting and staring at this apparition with the dark, fear-dilated eyes I thought we'd left behind in the City.

The agent spread his hands, and his wide white smile was enough to warn me. I yanked back on the reins, reaching stupidly for where my statrifle would have been on my own saddle, my fingers closing on empty air because my favorite fourpad had been vaporized.

Shit. Time to get creative.

Geoff made no sound when I hit. I tried to be gentle, both of us down and rolling into a manky, close side-passage. Vines shuddered as I tumbled over them, my arms and legs a cage around a child's thinness. Half-rotted cloth ripped, my shirt and utility vest shredding against the abrasive husks.

Get some height. What the hell are those mods in his profile?

Now my scans were alive with movement. I hadn't heard them before because they were agents in basemode, and they were all . . . strange.

The commchatter, part of it thick datastreams, sharpened as I launched myself, Geoff clinging to my neck and resin-windows shattering. They were everywhere, encrypted and not, the entire township-sized structure resonating with sonic wash to pinpoint my location and fog my scans.

"I dreamed him!" Geoff screamed into my neck. *"I dreamed him, Mommy!"*

We're going to have to talk about that. Just hang on a second. The fourpads could shift for themselves. If I could just get high enough, I could get through a section of the Trapp field that wasn't locked-down from stat discharge—

BOOM.

Falling. Arms and legs suddenly numb. Curled around Geoff, a thin shell for such a precious thing, *what the hell was that? Sonic, plas, what*?

It burrowed inside my head, overwhelming intake feeds and shorting out reflex loops. Another *crunch* as I hit the ground and the pain, great swelling breakers of it, nanos trying to cope with disaster, emergency sealing and repair.

Too slow. I was healing too fucking *slowly.*

"Careful." Footsteps, too light or heavy to be just-plain-warmbody. Why wasn't I healing? "This one's a hellion." A short, unamused chuckle. "Give her a jolt if she starts again."

"Abbymom?" Geoff's whisper. *"Mom?"*

Nano reset pulse. Ouch. It was a relief to figure out what had happened—a focused magno-lectric pulse, from a piece of Agency-strength tech. The first iterations of nanos were prone to going a little weird, and the resets were needed every month or so to keep everything functioning and the agent tumor-free. That didn't happen anymore, and when you were buffered a pulse wouldn't kill you.

It would only incapacitate you for a little while. Already my nanos were shaking off the reset, each one a star in the river of constellations that made up *me*. Each one spreading the message—*hey, we're not in a stasis tank, we're fine, pass the word along, will you? Let's get back to work.*

Agents. Closing in. Footsteps—the agent in the black hat. *Caught in a bad holo. Emergency measures.*

Arms and legs shaky, with only warmbody strength. Bones creaking as the nanos shook off lethargy and swarmed. A low humming under the noise of the Trapp field locking down again—were the idiots outside still firing at it? Morons. Where was Sam?

I levered myself up, my ribs snapping out and remolding themselves, a gout of clear red-tinged liquid coughing from my nose and mouth, all over my front like a drunken hax-sniffer's bib of vomitus. Geoff's fingers plucking weakly at me—he was trying to help.

I pushed him behind me. He didn't resist. I swayed, a flood of adrenaline triggering other emergency cascades. *Fight or flight? Can't run like this.*

Guess it's fight.

Blood dripping in my eyes, nanos diving back under my skin to continue their work. Faithful little silver motes, crawling all through me. *Sorry, that was a bad hit. Let's see what we can do.*

"Geoff," I croaked.

"Mama?" So small, his dry little voice.

"If they put me down, *run*."

"I don't want to leave you," he whispered.

"Do as I say." I pushed myself up straighter, scans coming back online, flicking through alternatives inside my head. Combat capability at a ridiculously low percentage, but I'd had worse odds before, hadn't I?

Not really.

All the tech, all the implementation, all the struggle and dead bodies and planning for contingencies, and in the end, a simple pulse was going to take me down.

I took a half-step forward. The other agents drew back, a collective movement. Kind of a compliment. Black Hat examined me.

He had a cruel sharp nose, cream-pale skin, flat silvery oculars, and a flat unamused mouth. No moss on him, no rotting. All of them were dry, and they all had the same silver eyes as the agents in New Vega. The same weird modding on their nanoprofiles, too. They all *moved* the same way—when Black Hat tensed, they followed suit, and when he moved, their balance shifted slightly. Those terrible blank oculars all focused on me, and I had the sudden weird idea that I was being examined not by a bunch of agents, but by one organism with several different eyes.

And hands.

"I'm going to make this simple," Black Hat said, and pointed. Not at me, but *past*. "I want the kid."

I had to clear my throat, and the crowd moved forward a few paces again. Where had they all been hiding?

Doesn't matter. I made sure each one of them could hear me, nice and loud, no subaudible grumbling here. It was a proverb popular both in-City and out, because it expressed a basic philosophical truth.

"Want in one hand, shit in the other. See which fills up first."

He showed his teeth, a horrid wide triangular peelback of those thin lips, and he probably would have jumped me. I was braced for it, ready, but another voice intruded.

"Careful." Sam stepped out of the shadows at the rear of the crowd. His clothes were in rags, same as mine, and he looked like he'd been rolled across the jungle floor a few times. "*He* wants her alive."

"*He* can go fuck himself," Black Hat spat.

Sam shrugged. "Why don't you say that to *his* face, then?"

Now. Do it now, while they think you're weak.

I lunged, my bladed hand crunching in the throat of the closest silver-eyed agent. Hooking and ripping, a gout of blackish blood full of silver motes swarming in an unfamiliar pattern.

Then my handler shot me. Or rather, he lifted a familiar black dial-box, and thumbed the switch while pointing the wand end at me. Another nano reset pulse crashed into me, and I went down hard.

CHAPTER ELEVEN

BLACK HAT COLLECTIVE

They came from below.

It wasn't any sort of Libera. It was just a shell, and it was clean because it was a decoy, a façade built over the entrance, booby-trapped and full of nasty surprises for anyone stupid enough to mount an assault. The Trapp field could lose the three above-ground generator-vents and still seal the entrance doors; there were secondary vents hidden away.

Hide, Sam had said. *Don't go below.*

I began to surface about two and a half minutes after he'd hit me with the second pulse. Restraints—not flexcable either. You can't immobilize an agent for more than a short while, we're just too good at wriggling. But a good way to stretch that little while out is with a cram-cradle. Wrists and ankles bound, chained together with cinchfilaments and then roped to each other with more cinchfil, your elbows, knees, ribs, hips, and head caged too. The harder you pull, the less give there is. Then sheets of cramwrap, round and round, a swaddling robbing the agent of everything but a few centimeters of breathing space. Struggle, and the wrap tightens, cutting off your air and sending you into anaerobic reserve mode.

Uncomfortable, to say the least.

I came back online in bits and pieces, being carried down a long ramp. For a moment I thought I was back in the city again, in the critical second stage of implementation, gliding on a gurney through the bowels of one of the black cubes.

Wait. I'm already implemented. Am I being upgraded? What the hell?

Each tiny bump made the wrap constrict a little. I couldn't get enough air in, and hovered between reserve mode and waking, struggling to cycle up. Little flashes, almost-dreams, on the half-lit border between consciousness and the soft fuzz of anaerobic.

Geoff, biting his lip a little as he concentrated on the water-maker. His head upflung, testing the wind, moonlight turning his young face into an adult's for a single weary moment.

Sam on the other side of the tank wall, his face unreadable as I floated. He'd come by to check on me during upgrades, and often stood there watching, turned into a green ghost by the restraint gel or tinted blue by the narcofluid. Sam splayed in the sand, limbs akimbo, watching me contain Geoff's struggles. What was that look on his face? There and gone in less than a heartbeat.

"He *wants her alive.*"

Who?

Flash after flash—running rooftops, dodging fire, the cold scrape-burning between my legs as I stared into a clinic's harsh lamplight overhead, the cocktails of drugs and hypno to prep me for the first stages of implementation. The second, critical stage where the neural reshaping takes place, nanos differentiating and multiplying, a hyperalloy bath crackling with lectric force as the little things formed chains to reinforce bones, reshape muscles, make me stronger, faster, smarter. The third phase is all delicate work, fine-tuning metabolism and cycling parameters, making sure the nanos have the complex mélange of chemicals, metals, minerals, and proteins they need to finish implementation. Jolts of concentrated sucrose, glucose, tanch-rymose, all sorts of vat-grown proteins—it takes a lot of energy to keep a body functioning through such invasive restructuring.

It was enough to make you wonder if you were the same person when you woke up, sore as hell and with twitchy trigger reflexes. Short courses of sedation while you're taught to control your new body, hypno from the prep locking into place and making sure you don't kill the warmbody support staff or accidentally walk through a wall. Learning to cycle effectively, how to conserve your energy, how to deal with basic biological necessities becoming nothing but amenities. How to pass for warmbody. The temperature fluctuations—until you learn to normalize, the bone-reinforcing can make you feel cold. Even after you find your norm physically, there's the psychological impacts. Sometimes the coldness doesn't go away.

You're a machine. You're Agency property. You are owned, and you will do your job or you will be Dismissed.

Finding out that being able to throttle your autonomics didn't mean you didn't *feel* it. The Dismissal rate spikes, we were told, between the first six and eight months after implementation. That spike is spurred by purely psychological degradation; even the best testing beforehand won't show where an agent might go off the rails in those first few months.

After that, the Dismissal rate declines to near zero—but the threat never goes away.

The jostling stopped. The cramwrap relaxed a little as I was laid on a flat surface, and I heard the humming of a grav-gurney. So familiar.

Their eyes. Their nanoprofiles. Something there. Oxygen crept back in, I hovered on the borderline a little longer, then woke fully when the cramwrap was fractionally loosened again. Not enough, but at least I could breathe, and my nanos went into overdrive.

My vision sharpened. The bouncing, effervescent sound in the corridor was the vibrations of the Trapp generator. Did they live with that all the time, humming in their bones?

Sam walked alongside the gurney. Four of the silver-oculared agents surrounded us, as if they were warmbody scientists and support staff accompanying a new agent. Their voices wavered, reaching me in bursts through the hum and my intake feeds fuzzing intermittent as I tried to shake off reserve mode.

Just let the nanos work.

Geoff. Where was he?

Aural intake blazed back into life. "—not going to be happy about this." Sam, in one of his more patently reasonable, negotiating tones.

"That is beyond our control." A female silver-eyed agent, the words passionless and uninflected even more than a facilitator's just-passing-the-news-along.

"Sure it is, but if the Collective tries to implement her, we'll lose a resource. And she's a newer model, you might not be able to—"

"Too dangerous." Male, now, from my left. Strangely, it was the same voice, the same tone, but filtered through a different throat's dimensions. "Must be contained. You are useful. Do not press."

Sam didn't miss a beat. "You can understand my hesitation. I'm the one who has to take the news back."

"The others have been captured. All is according to plan." Another male, down near my feet instead of at my head. Again, same voice, different throat.

I ran the differences in the nanoprofile through my head again. Glucose levels in my brain spiked, almost shutting down my precarious hold on consciousness.

The differences weren't really the odd thing. The odd thing was the overlapping similarity in each agent's profile. Introducing your nanos into another agent will trigger a war between the two, the host's body the battleground, and the invaders will die a swift death.

They replicate, sure, and you don't run out of them . . . but it's not pleasant to think about losing a massive number of the colony that makes you better.

Wait. Don't look at that, look at the—

Driven into anaerobic again. I surfaced a bare thirty seconds later according to chrono, and spent a few moments getting as much oxygen as I could without triggering the wrap.

"Whose plan? No, I don't want to know. I'm just a messenger, guys."

"You have your part." The female again. "You are useful."

It's not the nanoprofiles at all. They're outside parameters. Measurements not even close to optimal, not even close to baseline.

That had been nagging at me ever since I'd tangled with the silver-eyed bastards in New Vega. Their measurements just hadn't been right, and the satisfaction of figuring *that* out was only deep enough to make everything else that much grimmer.

These people shouldn't have been implemented at all, and doubly shouldn't have survived the process. Which meant . . . what? So hard to think when each fresh burst of brain activity threatened to shut me down into reserve again.

"Thanks." A touch of grim amusement. Sam didn't look down at me—I could only see him in quarter-profile.

"We are here." The second male spoke, and a rosy light bloomed through my eyelashes. The gurney bumped just a little, and the wrap choked up again, but not before a faint, horrible idea occurred to me.

They have nanos, all right. They're not agents? The measurements . . .

The Collective.

Swimming up again. A stinging all over me. Voices.

"—fighting the sedation. How is that possible?" That same voice, this time through a younger throat, its shades and nuances of individuality not yet erased.

"The will commands, the body obeys." Black Hat, sounding grimly amused. "Leave us."

"Sir?"

"Leave us."

Sound of movement. Sam's voice, then, swimming through the layers of gauze and wrap holding me down. "I'm not going anywhere."

"I didn't tell *you* to. They're useful, but we don't want them getting ideas." A slight ticking—the sound of a controlled drip. Chemical stink, familiar but I couldn't quite place it. "Besides, you'll want to make sure we don't put any tiny gifts in this prize for your owner."

"Glad you understand, and you're not going to implement." A bitter, sardonic edge I'd never heard Sam deploy before. "You do realize *he* wanted the kid too?"

"Fine. Take the kid, and we'll keep this one."

Silence.

"I thought so." Black Hat laughed like a drug dealer doublecrossing a decoy runner. "How are you going to explain this to *him*?"

"That's my problem. Hullo, Jess."

Blinking, slowly. The dripping was sedation tubes, the standard five-tower complement. I couldn't see past them and a circle of red glow I was trapped in. My tongue had turned thick and slow.

I still managed a word. "Bastard."

They drew closer, the shadows looming over me. Black Hat's irises were luminous, the pupils vertical slits, fine silvery threads all through the white. Not the flat metallic orbs the others had. Was that why he sounded like himself, and the others were all one voice?

His voice?

My scans were completely nonfunctional. The nanos were struggling to keep me conscious.

Sam, still in rags and covered with crusted blood, sap, and various other things, smiled at me. It was a rather gentle, diffuse beaming, strange on his thinner-than-in-the-City face. "Nice to see you too."

"Young love." Black Hat's snigger grated across my nerves. The stinging was the sedation lulling my nanos, a chemical restraint. Sooner or later the little silver motes would eat through it, and bring me fully online. Then I could figure out getting free of the wrap. "Jess, is it?"

No, it's not. "Who . . . are you?" I sounded drunk. A few times in my warmbody youth I'd gotten wasted on water-clear glivorny; this was the same slurring, the same pause, the tongue not obeying.

"We are Rebellion." The thin lips lingered over the word, almost lovingly. "We are *Collective*."

Great. That doesn't tell me a fucking thing I didn't already guess, you holotale bastard. I could feel my face moving, unmoored from my control. What was my expression giving away?

"She doesn't look impressed." Sam, helpfully. I didn't glance at him.

There would be a point, very soon, when I'd talk to him up close. It would be a short conversation, and when it was done, his head would not only be separated from his body, but I'd find something that could destroy an agent's braincase. It might take me a while, but I'd figure it out.

It was what I would call *worth the fucking effort*.

Black Hat shrugged. "We could flood her with our little friends. She would be an asset, once we finished. Such dedication."

Sam made a slight movement. Was it a shrug? "The risk of failure is about eighty percent with the new models. More importantly, this would also conclude our business relationship in a very unsatisfactory fashion."

I made my mouth move again. *I know who you are.* "Nikor." *Not a real man. Nikor's a myth. Was this man just using his name?*

They both stilled, an agent's uncanny quiescence.

Black Hat gazed at me. The dripping kept going, each little drop another brick landing on me. I finally placed the chemical smell filling my nostrils.

Restraint gel. And a lot of it. How do they have that here? Where do they get this tech?

Black Hat decided it was time to pontificate a little. "The Cities are dying. The corporations are strangling each other. Liberation is around the corner." That stretched smile, spreading those thin lips. "When we harvest the zero-gen, the Collective will spread. Tell me . . ." A pressure on the wrap, faint and faraway. He was stroking my belly. "What would you give, to have a child of your own? A *true* one, not that facsimile? We could make it happen."

You motherfucking piece of shit. "My . . . kid . . . Fuck . . . you." *I am going to kill you, too. You can't hold me forever.*

"Charming." Polishing the wrap over my belly, rubbing it in small circles. "You're angry. So am I. Don't you want to burn their world down? Didn't they lie to you, the same way they lied to me? *You're a machine. You're expendable. You belong to the Agency now.*"

"Collective." I croaked. "Just like . . . a corporation." *You are what you hate, didn't Barlowe always say that? "You are what you hate, Sara, so be careful."* Why he called me "Sara" I never knew.

Barlowe's body hanging from the railprobe, a good clean sudden death.

The agent-implemented don't inadvertently blush. Still, his face twisted and darkened, and I realized, with a certain chemically blunted satisfaction, that I was seeing rage so intense a subroutine couldn't clamp it.

Good.

Black Hat stilled again, his expression smoothing out. Sam didn't move, but I could *feel* his tension. If Black Hat wanted to Dismiss me, now was the time, and it would force Sam into doing . . . what?

Probably nothing.

Hate is stupid. Even some agents don't ever figure that out. They think *practically invulnerable* means *go ahead and waste resources*. Plus, you're never going to earn your way out of the Agency's investment in you and subsequent upgrades, so some don't bother being frugal. *Already owned, might as well use it.* They let petty one-upmanship and vendettas bloom.

The *real* reason not to hate is just that it's so *inefficient*. It lets things slip, like the fact that one of my ragged nails had been working at the bottom of the cramwrap steadily now, picking and shearing a few molecular strands at a time. The longer I could keep him talking, the more chance I had of making some sort of move, even with the sedation. *Just put your head down and get the job done*. Like waiting, it was the most efficient way, but also the slowest.

"A pity we won't keep her." Black Hat was back to sardonic. "Smart *and* vicious. I almost envy you."

"Can the Collective envy?" Sam sounded only mildly

interested. I focused up past them, at the glaring, ruddy light—neon tubes, just like in the Cirquit or the Projekts. In-City they were blue, because that was a soothing color. A cold color, too, to keep people shivering and turning their thermservers up. Red was too dangerous to bathe a whole population in. "Or is it just a warmbody response?"

"They feel nothing." Black Hat's fingers sharpened, digging into my midriff. My slight movement, dragging the sharp broken point of one fingernail through the cramwrap at just the right angle, didn't cease. He'd probably think it a nerve oscillation. "The burden is mine. Would she share it, if we took hold?"

Sam shrugged, filthy cloth rasping and flapping slightly. "The weight of rule, old man. Let's get this over with."

"You prefer to be aboveground." Another bitter little laugh. "Very well. Goodbye, Jess. Sweet dreams."

Anger is inefficient, too. So is flailing. My mouth opened, but anything I could have said was drowned as the sedation spiked and the gurney tipped. No numbpatch—had Sam had it for this moment, and used it early?

So I was awake when they tipped me into the restraint tank. Burning on faraway drowsing nerves, time slowing down, the thick green fluid closing over my head, the reflex of holding a breath irresistible because when it ended and my body expelled the air, the gel would slide down my throat, fill my lungs, and suffocating, trying to breathe, trying to *breathe*—

Mercifully, I grayed into anaerobic reserve mode. It didn't halt the inevitable.

I drowned.

Green glow. A vertical restraint tank is a tube of shatter-resistant plasilca; it cradles and cushions. The cramwrap dissolving in floating gauze veils, so slowly. Time stretches, slows, limbs heavy and clumsy with sleep. Just enough oxygen and glucose to keep you right above shutdown, and the veils of chemical restraint turn the nanos all the way down. Pulse, respiration, metabolism all throttled back to deepcycle norms. It's not like a stasis tank, blissful oblivion floating in blue narcofluid. This was for the treatments that required an agent to still have some baseline activity, not the absolute blankness of stasis.

The worst part was trying to *think*. Urgency pressing on me, the soupy half-sense of something wrong, struggling against the weight. Shadows moving outside the tube—the pressure equalized and I floated, veils of dirt, sap, dried blood unwinding too as the gel passed through the corelli filters and returned.

I'm in a tank. Something happened. Am I upgrading?

The gel tasted wrong. Agency restraint gel actually *has* no taste. This had a bitter green undertone.

Trees. The trees are part of it.

Trees? The Ring and the suburbs had them, with statrepellers to keep the soot and pollution off. I'd crouched in one, moving with the limbs, a camo-suit blurring my outline, as I watched a group of—

Little boy, dark hair and a scar on his chin . . .

—of schoolchildren walking home.

Hey freak! A flung stone, the taunting. The child's thin shoulders, defeated and yet somehow expressing arrogance . . .

There had been a job. A restaurant full of fauxsmoke, and the brown paper envelope. Sam across the table. *I don't do kid jobs,* I told him.

The important thing I had to do floated with me, just out of reach. Restraint gel does funny things to your perceptions. The two shadows in the room outside faded, and the light was wrong too. Agency restraint bays are lit with cold clinical white-bars, pitilessly exposing every stain and crack in the world.

I'm not in the City.

My body knew better than I did. My left hand, now free of cramwrap, curled slowly, so slowly, into a fist. Pressure against my wrists.

Restraints. Why cinchfilament? That's not right.

A flash—a pair of big, wounded dark eyes. A salt-hot, concentrated smell. Soft, fragile warmbody arms around my neck.

The cinches loosened, restraint gel easing them away. Even cinchfil gives up under the gel. Fuzzy awareness of something important, something *critical*, fighting through the haze.

I saw it on a holo. You don't have to.

Pressing my lips to the curve of a fragile skull, and that *smell*. Of all the scents in the world, that one reached through the restraint gel and pulled on me, made my left fist curl even more tightly. The cinchfilament on that wrist was almost eaten away, and my arm started to bend, lifting, lifting.

Reserve glucose. Emergency directive to the nanos, struggling against the sleepy warmth. Concentrate.

One of the shadows came back. Just at the edge of my perceptions. Dangerous, but I had to try.

Why? What's so important? You're in restraint, probably because a job went sideways . . .

Light. Not outside, but *inside* my head. A plasma ball, searing-bright, and the brain activity ate up a significant part of the glucose stocks I needed.

Geoff. They have him. Harvest, that motherfucker said. The nanos . . .

The whole thing trembled inside my skull, and the realization that followed tightened my left fist even further. My arm was drifting, elbow almost near my ear—difficult to gauge distances, proprioception off because the gel had varying resistances. Had to account for that, if I intended . . .

Don't worry about the nanos. Don't worry about the Collective. It's simple. They have your kid.

Floating. The gel began to eat at the rags of sodden, rotting cloth on me. That was the green tint in the taste. The sap, throwing off the chemical balance needed to keep me completely passive. *Use it, then. Work fast.*

Except I couldn't work fast. Hurrying would disturb the glucose harboring, and the gel would resist more the faster I moved.

They have your kid.

Strange. Floating, concentrating, the realization flooding me with clarity for a single moment. I wasn't being efficient. Not anymore.

Anger wastes energy. So does hatred.

But *they had my kid.*

Sooner or later, there is a place beyond rage.

My arm drifted up further, and I braced myself.

Geoff needs you.

Get out of here.

Hanging in the restraint gel, I twitched.

Thud.

The long slow cycle begins again. Drawing back the arm, beginning the glucose harboring procedure again. The green taste fading and flaring as the restraint gel filtered and refreshed itself, bitter almost-freedom replaced with tasteless sludge and concurrent blunting of any mental acuity. The gel's meant to give you some rest, especially if you've had the shock of dismemberment. Of course you know the nanos will seal you up until you can be put together . . . but your body doesn't. The same stupid warmbody response that fills you with fear during combat doesn't understand nanos. It only understands millennia of that ripping and tearing as meaning death, an end to all striving.

Thud. Draw the arm back again, begin the conservation of glucose and mental effort.

A star-shaped blemish in the plasilca tube, cracking from pressure it was never meant to contain. Complicated equations—fast enough to pierce the gel, slowly enough that the fluid wouldn't constrict me, waiting until close enough and pow, the effort causing a blank spot inside my head as my arm used all the reserved stores of glucose.

If they had a tech monitoring my vitals they might notice a pattern. It was a risk.

Would they care? They had what they wanted—

My kid. They have my kid.

Past rage. Past fear. The place where you make a simple decision. Where complexity has been stripped away, and all that remains is your fist, drifting forward, getting closer, and—

Thud.

The star-blemish widened. Tiny threads of restraint gel oozed through it to splatter down in streaks. Not fast enough, and the green taste was fading. With it, my chances of staying conscious long enough to work my way free dimmed.

Didn't matter.

My arm drifted back, again.

Thud.

And again.

Thud.

CHAPTER TWELVE

WHO OWNS YOU NOW?

Fading bitterness coating the tongue. Concentration guttering, a candleflame under monsoon assault. Chrono useless, no attention to spare for it anyway. Reserve the glucose, drift the arm up, drift it forward so slowly, then, the punch. The breakage-star widened, and a steady stream of restraint gel oozed out, steaming as it hit the air outside.

A shadow moved outside the tank. Doubled, tripled, or maybe it was just my perceptions blurring. The sap contamination had all but leached out of the tank now, caught in the corelli filters, and the gel level wasn't dropping quickly enough and the times between punches were stretching.

Running out of time. The shadow loomed closer, warped outside the column. Was someone standing there watching me—

WHAM.

The world turned over, a wet gushing, tearing sound. Sudden pressure-release, my body a thrown toy, a doll with heavy limbs. Blackness swallowed me, and the sense of falling, shrieking inwardly—had they figured out what I was doing? Sealed the tank and flooded me with near-toxic sedation again? Was I even now in a transport hold, carried further and further from Geoff, rocking in a narcofluid bath, conscious and screaming but unable to breathe?

Time is a subjective thing, even when you have built-in chrono. It felt like forever, but it was probably only twenty seconds of thrashing, the freezing metal grating scraping weals on my gel-slick skin, before my body brought up all the fluid in my lungs and stomach, expelling it from every orifice with a massive cramping.

Normally they keep you sedated while they drain restraint gel, and administer a slow system flush so you come online just like cycling up out of deep gamma into theta and above slowly and naturally. It means you don't flop around like a clonetank fish pulled out for gene-testing.

Restraints. Only they weren't cinchfilament or cramwrap. Just two of them, hyperalloy bars with a softer covering. Noise, shrieking through every aural intake channel, red light and a welter of sensation.

"It's all right," he kept repeating. "It's okay, Je—ah, Abby. It's okay. Shhhh."

Retching. More cramping. Nanos shocked back into life, the whole colony scattering like a herd of frightened fourpads—

Not in the City. Restraint gel. Had me in a tube. I coughed up a last gout of gel, nanos swarming my lungs and heart, checking for damage, eating waste and toxins, normalizing metabolism but so slowly. Autonomics crazy but no energy for subroutines, I finally went limp, dragging in knife-sharp air and moaning.

"It's all right," he repeated. "It's okay. I've got you."

Bastard. Oh you bastard. Just wait. I didn't waste any breath saying it. Gel dried, crackling all over me. No clothes. No weapons.

I'd make do.

I heaved myself away from Sam, or I tried to. Until the nanos could finish, I was only warmbody-strong. Ridiculous to think I could hurt an agent, but I thrashed around and got a good solid punch to his cheek. His head tipped back slightly, but he just looked down his nose at me.

So I hit him again. And again.

Muscle movement makes the toxins float around. I needed a system flush and a half-standard hour to let the nanos work. I suspected I wasn't going to get either.

"Calm down." And *fuck* if Sam didn't sound calm. And a little amused, too.

I'm going to wipe that right off your face. I am going to Dismiss you, motherfucker.

Patience. He could wait, I couldn't. *Geoff. Where is he?*

A sticky wave of restraint gel washed across the metal grating serving as a floor. It was an agent's medbay, the tech old but reliable—restraint tubes, gel mixers, piles of familiar bio-canisters. Baremetal stripchairs with high-arched spider-arms holding sharp edges and long capped syringes, now *those* belonged in a museum.

I went absolutely still. Dragged in a deep breath, coughed again. A scouring pain inside my lungs. I spat a wad of partially processed gel, it splatted dully against the flooring and I immediately felt much better.

Which meant I heaved away from Sam and actually managed to untangle myself this time. Or he let me go. I made it to hands and knees, surged upright, and fell against the restraint console, scraping my hip and almost opening my scalp in a long line as I slid on numb-tingling gel. The shit was *everywhere*, and sending up a nosewatering stench as it decayed.

"You need a system flush, Abby. Then we can get you out of here."

"Don't. Call. Me. That." I tried again, fell again. Body just wouldn't obey. The nanos were working, but they needed time.

Time I didn't have.

"At first I wondered why you picked *that* name. Most agents never go back to their original, even camouflaged." He rocked up into a loose easy crouch, barely wrinkling his nose at the smell. Loose-fitting dark navy shocktrooper gear, strange to see on my handler. He was usually clad in a rumpled suit or more recently in faded, frayed odds and ends to blend with the desert.

If I could incapacitate him, I could take at least some of the clothes. The boots wouldn't fit me, but I'd make it work.

I had to.

"Then I figured it out. My girl, my little stone-cold killer, my favorite flex liquidator, just had to have somewhere to hang all her frustrated feelings. You play it so close. You always have."

Keep talking. I grabbed onto the console. Fingers slipping in gel, nanos fighting the numbing as well as the toxins. *See if I care.* I hauled, a short sound of effort escaping me.

A warmbody grunt. Weak, and stupid, and useless. Right now, though, it was all I had.

Scans started to come online, patchy and rough, handicapped by no available energy and also by the thunderous fuzz of the Trapp core. Now I was hoping that all the rest and relaxation I'd been in the habit of giving my nanos was going to pay off. That they would be fresh and ready to fight, so to speak.

"I've got a system flush for you, Abby. And while they're occupied, we'll slip out. I don't trust that motherfucker as far as I can—"

I spat another wad of processed gel. It hit him square in the face, and I concentrated on pulling myself up. If I could just get vertical, maybe I could balance. From there, the rest would be easy. I would find wherever they had Geoff, and if he was hurt, if they had done something to my kid . . .

Well. I could crawl, and I could kill. It would have to be enough.

Sam wiped his cheek, solemn. A long pause.

I made it to my feet. Hooked my fingers around a transvital lever, ground my implemented teeth together as I focused on standing upright.

The world turned over again.

"So fucking stubborn." A heavy sigh. "I can carry you out of here."

I looked up at the console. There had to be something I could use to keep myself upright.

Fuck it. I spasmed onto hands and knees. Drying gel peeled off me in sheets. I closed my eyes, hair hanging down, dripping fat plopping pieces of almost-liquid. *First step, getting out of this hole. Then scanning for Geoff. Or getting one of those silver-eyed bastards and making it tell me where he is.*

I began to crawl.

"Shit." The shocktrooper gear creaked slightly as Sam rose. "Why won't you let me help you?"

You bastard. "Geoff." It was all I said. *My kid.*

"He'll serve a purpose taking down the Collective. And seriously, sweets, did you really think I'd let them have you too? You give me *more* trouble, Abby."

"Fuck . . . you." *Don't waste your time talking.*

"Since we're both implemented, we'll probably have to express our affection in other ways." He was close, but I ignored him. Something wondrous had occurred.

I'd seen stairs. Going *up*.

"But for you, I'll certainly try my best." He sighed again, and his foot flicked out, taking my arm out from under me. Before I could fall he was on me, and I struggled as a spear of ice buried itself in my right glute.

A familiar warmth spread from it, though, and I froze.

System flush? What?

"Listen to me," he whispered, hot breath in my ear. His arms were hyperalloy bars again, but as soon as the flush spread and consumed the toxins, I'd be strong again too. "I am about to fuck up my entire *existence* for you, Jess-Abby-sweetheart, whatever you want me to call you. So *listen*."

I kept still. The warmth spread, down my right leg. The most useless place to stick a system flush in, of course. He wanted me incapacitated for just a little longer.

"There's more players in the game than you realize. Corporations, Agency, Nikor and his alliance, some of the bigger townships. All of them want *this* crazy motherfucker dusted, but not before they get specs on what he's done. Those silver-eyed bastards are warmbodies infected with all-purpose nanos. He made the Collective real."

I couldn't help myself. "Another fairytale." It made sense. Their specs weren't even close to implementation norms. And those voices—all one voice, from several throats.

His voice.

Collective . . . we will spread. We will burn the world down.

"Whatever. In any case, he was a warmbody genius too, and the Agency's salivating to get their hands on his process. I have the specs, I could walk out of here while you're keeping them busy. Secondary directive was erasing the Collective, and that's what your little friend is for. He's poison bait, only that bastard Paxton had to go above and beyond. Couldn't help himself, we don't even know *what* he did or where he found whatever he spliced in to make the kid. You were the best bet to get our bait out of town. And then you had to go get attached."

It finally made sense. "I'm going to kill you," I whispered.

He let go of me. The warmth was crawling up my naked back, spreading rapidly now as the nanos recognized the chemprofile and began utilizing it.

"We can sell the specs, Abby." Quiet and reasonable. "You and me, anywhere in the world. There's so many things you don't even know about."

You know, that might have sounded halfway appetizing before you turned out to be an absolute fuckwad. "Where. Is. Geoff?"

Another long pause. Soon, very soon, the flush would be complete. Tendrils of heat creeping up my back, a fire lit in my belly, masses of nanos swarming.

"They're going to try to add him to the Collective, they don't know his gene matrix will eat theirs alive and kill the nanos as well. He's prepped for harvest. They've already administered an eliminex round to get the sap and the narco-mist out of his—*ulp*!"

Even if it's just your legs that can work, you can do what you need to. I swept his feet from under him, losing skin all up my right side, and knotted my fingers in his hair. The flush, propelled by muscles firing, exploded through my torso. We were nose-to-nose again, Sam and I. I had time to study every fine thread of pigment in his irises up close, time to breathe in his breath.

"*Where?*" A harsh, guttural syllable, right at the lowest range I could produce audibly. It tore out of my raw throat, but he didn't blink. He just stared into my eyes as well. Was he memorizing my irises? Did he see anything behind my pupils, some spark even implementation couldn't capture?

He told me. I let go of him, closed my eyes, shook my weakened arms. My side burned, skin swiftly healing. Nothing excreting through any pore or orifice, though, the nanos eating toxins and leftover sedation to fuel me.

Up the stairs, agent. Get moving.

I got to work.

Every township or district has an underside, and it's there I usually end up. Liquidators work best under the surface. Little subdermal conveyers of havoc, it was what we were made for.

I was deep underground, the thumping of the Trapp core working its way into every muscle and bone, grimy dark tunnels lit with red, no litter or waste in sight. There were statrepellers to take care of the dust, probably cycling through daily but dead and dark right now. The tech in the warren was old but serviceable, again, and it made me wonder how Black Hat had pulled off the trick of making nanos that didn't need implementation parameters.

Of course, an agent retains higher brain function, and has functional immortality. The implementation parameters are there to ensure both. Without, you get tumor-ridden death or complete shock as the process destabilizes the physical matrix beyond repair.

Or, you get . . . *them*. Many eyes, many hands, but one voice. The first experiments with nanos, in the dim last days of the Gene Wars, had produced brain-melted, creeping automatons that eventually succumbed under the weight of fast-growing tumors—cell division run amok, personalities shredding, no shutoff protocols or balance equations. They taught you as much in primary school, explaining why full implementation wouldn't work for everyone, and that's why it took me so long to remember. Everything before I woke up implemented is . . . darker, less easy to access.

I'd only had warmbody senses then.

Black Hat had been an agent, maybe, and his own nanos kept the other crop of little bastards in check? Who knew? I didn't care to figure it out just now.

I was too occupied staying out of sight. Clinging to pipes on the roof of the tunnels, feet on either side and my thighs burning as the splits stressed knees and hip joints in novel ways. Underneath me, a group of almost-agents moved in lockstep, without even scanning their environs. My own scans were minimal, to keep from alerting them. The system flush was doing its work, but impatience beat behind my reinforced breastbone. Eliminex round meant they were ready to start surgically harvesting.

Maybe Geoff could heal like the second-gens. But alone and afraid, strapped to a table and dissected . . . no.

No.

Muscling through the tops of corridors, clinging to pipes to dodge discovery, hoping Sam hadn't lied one final time just to twist the knife. Hoping I hadn't lost too much time before he used whatever he'd picked up to break me out of the restraint tube. He could have just started the cooldown process and administered the system flush—but he'd wanted me vulnerable.

Weak. Why?

Don't care. Don't want to care either. Move.

Creeping naked through the red neon glow, the flakes of gel rubbed free of my skin, I ghosted through Libera's eerily clean tubes. Comchatter and short-e bounced around, only one or two streams encrypted now, the rest a tangle of feedback and information. I could, possibly, tune a couple streams and drop into them, just like hacking an uplink or a corporate system. It wouldn't do anything, there was too much raw data bouncing around. No voices, though. They must have used audible just to lure me in.

The tunnels sloped further down. A black heart beating in the center of the Collective, the Trapp core close enough to start fuzzing the edges of scanrange with its flux-heart.

Except the heart wasn't truly black. The closer I got to that diseased cardiac chamber, the more the red tubes were bleached by proper lighting. A soft forgiving rosy pink bathed each metal surface instead, and the tech was sleeker. There were a few countermeasures that wouldn't be out of place in-City, but they were at least a year old.

Child's play. Except I was child-weak, and the system flush couldn't give me extra calories to burn. It was warmer than usual, the therms were free energy, but I couldn't afford to gobble them and alert everyone with a huge cold spot over their heads.

What exactly are you going to do, agent? Look at you. No gear, no clothes, working off possibly bad intel and weak as a fluorox sniffer after a three-day bender. Pathetic.

Finally, the mess of pipes and cables overhead ended. I had to drop a few meters down, hit a catwalk, skirt a bulge of sheeting that, from the heat it threw off, was a geothermal feed, and get through a scanlocked door of blank metal.

I hung for a long moment, arms shaking as the flush finished burning through me and my nanos came fully online. Relief to feel the constellations inside me again, to scan for damage and decide I was operating at about forty percent capacity.

It has to be enough. Drop, and—wait.

I didn't drop. I jackknifed and wrapped my legs around a handy pipe, ignoring the burning. Another exhaust, but a cheap source of power, I squeezed my knees together and the nanos crowded, turning the skin inside my thighs to a heatsink, drinking in the excitement thrown off by dancing molecules.

My head hung back, my gel-filthy hair dried stiff. I heard a familiar silence in the space between ear and brain.

Commchatter began to burst around me, the data-streams tangling. A disharmony in the Collective's endless singing.

Screaming. Static. Feedback.

The second-gens had found a way through the Trapp field. Maybe they were after Geoff, or Sam. Either way, they were a welcome diversion. I hesitated, eyes closed, trying to track their progress with quiet, careful scanning.

Fuck it.

I dropped, my seared thighs giving a brief crackling flash into the visible spectrum as some of the heat bled off, and landed catfoot on the narrow strip of metal over an abyss. A hot draft rose from below—probably the Trapp core, or the geothermals that fueled its endless reactions.

Two ways to open a scanlocked door. You can kick it down, but that's often inefficient. Much easier if it just opens, because it thinks you're one of the hallowed few to pass it.

I didn't think this one would. I couldn't be that lucky.

You know you're just going to split yourself open on that thing. If you can get through you're going to be critically weakened. It's not worth it. Walk away.

I skipped back, eating up the distance to the end of the catwalk. Stairs spiraled up into bloody light.

Come on, agent. Walk away.

The door got bigger and bigger as I blurred through space. Maximum speed, efficient strides, skin erased from my bare feet on the grill of the walkway, the pain bright spikes through me as the nanos hummed, throwing endorphins into my bloodstream, thickening the tissue on my feet, bracing for impact, flashing adrenaline and cortisol to jack me into maximum combat readiness—or at least the maximum I could hope for in my current state.

I hit the door at full speed, and bounced off. Picked myself back up again, shaking the stunning noise out of my head, and was about to do it again, when it folded aside, lenticular layers blooming like a flower.

Oh. Well. That was simple. I limped forward and nipped through before it finished yawning.

Searing white light. Clean surfaces. For a moment the past looped over to eat the present and I was in an Agency lab, sleek white enamel and quiet humming statfields, brushers and sweepers to keep dust away from delicate implementation tools. The two spiderchairs here were much newer, arms tipped with up-to-the-minute edgers, punctures, stipplers, and other tools to sculpt tissue and inject chemical—and other—cocktails.

Most of the space was taken up with a massive fan-shaped control deck and an operating bay with a very modern, ultra-equipped medtable. The control deck's screens were alive with floating code and video streams, their flickers lost in the bright lighting.

A table that held a horizontal column of warmbody restraint gel, orange instead of green. Floating in it, naked, was a boy of about twelve, his dark hair moving gently on gel currents.

I let out an involuntary sound, scanned the room again. Empty. Streams of data moved over the control deck screens. I spent a moment studying them all, and the layout of the entire complex bloomed inside my head.

Bigger than I thought. This can't be the only implementation bay, there's too many of them for that. Ah, there, there, and there. Shit, there's a lot of them. Probably bare-bones ones, like where they had me. This is where the tech's concentrated.

Possible escape routes flashing through my braincase, I studied the controls on the medtable. Punched a few buttons and was rewarded with a soft gurgling and lights changing from green to red, a row of them marching from right to left. The gel began to drain. No reason to break the tube and make him sick—he could go into seizure like I did, and had no nanos to shield him from the shock.

The fuzzy thumping of the Trapp core blurred all my scans. It was annoying. I glanced at the screens again, straining to hear the datastreams and commchatter through the whitenoise.

Shrieks. Moans. The Collective agents could probably drag the second-gens down through sheer weight of numbers, and the complex terrain favored the defenders even if the second-gens could move fast enough.

Before they were dragged down, though, they would do quite a bit of damage. Did the entire Collective feel it when one of them was torn apart?

No sound, not even a whisper, but that same tickle in the place that warned me of Geoff's murderous cousins. The air pressure didn't change, but I was already throwing myself aside, so he blinked through the space where I'd been standing and crashed into the control deck. His hat flew off, his limbs contracting and the top of his head a silvery dome etched with strange whorls, lank hair in a fringe around the edges whipping as he blinked aside.

Fuck.

Forty percent combat capability and a pissed-off agent jacked up on who knew what mods? And Geoff in the tube, slowly waking up.

I was airborne, body reacting with the instinct of a thousand fights. Slammed into one of the spiderchairs, fingers curling around a trembling leg, pulling it free with a screech. Black Hat snarled, and I snarled back, not caring if it wasted energy. Subaudible growled as datastreams tangled—his followers were busy with the second-gens, he couldn't get them in here to overwhelm me. Good news.

Not for long. Come on, agent. Move.

The restraint tube was draining, but too slowly. Black Hat

leapt for me, I jabbed with the spiderleg and sprang for the control deck. Sparks flew, plasilca screens breaking, shrapnel piercing my thickening skin. The nanos could only do so much.

I kicked one of the control deck's processing towers. More sparks fountained, and Black Hat howled. He was fast even for an agent, stuttering through space to backhand me, sending me flying across the bay again.

Got his attention. Good. Does hitting the processing towers hurt him? Let's hope.

No time for hope. Balance gained, and he'd knocked me towards racks of biocanisters. Sleek silver City-stamped bullets, chemical codes lase-labeled on sides and ends.

All right, agent. Be smart.

I hit hard enough to knock two of the frames over, lashing out with the torn-free spiderchair arm. The Trapp core below pulsed, sending out a shrieking wail—*what the hell's that? Ignore it.*

Black Hat leapt, and everything slowed down. Time stretched, twisting and turning like the cheap tachmose candy runner kids chew. Get a mouthful of that good and soft, you can stick your fingers in and pull out a wad, stretch it into all sorts of shapes, loop it over your fingers, flick tiny bits of it into another kid's hair—if you thought that kid wouldn't try to shiv you over the prank, because once it hit hair it didn't come out unless you could wash in akketone.

Crack. Hit a sealed canister just right, and you can split it along a minute seam. Pierce another one with a lightning-quick jab, and you can have all sorts of fun.

Especially with warmbody restraint gel and unbuffered solachic acid.

I rolled aside, straining against gravity, exhaustion, time itself. Body failing, nanos in overdrive scraping at the last dregs of muscle reserves to get me *away*. Not so much from him, but from the flood of solachic splashing into the gel glugging out of its shattered container.

Even nanos have a limit. Arms failing, fingers slipping, Black Hat smashed into the widening orange stain behind me. It splashed and I let out a miserable cry of fear and agony mixed—burning droplets on my skin, a burst of foul smoke.

Yeah. You mix any kind of class B gel and solachic without a buffer, and you get big, ugly pool of nasty.

I fetched up against the second spiderchair, another stunning ringing inside my skull. *Move! Move, you stupid bitch! Move now!*

Couldn't. Grayed out, nanos swarming to protect vital organs. He was coming for me, the mad head of the Collective beast, and I couldn't lift a finger.

I swam in and out of consciousness for a short while, bursts of screaming static and a horrid wet bubbling filling my intake feeds in sporadic bursts. Slowly came online again, a soft familiar padding drawing closer.

"Abbymom?" A strangled sob. "Mommy?"

I'm here, I wanted to say. Couldn't make my mouth work. Breathing rapidly, ambient temperature dropping as I grabbed every scrap of energy available around me—therms, whatever—and forced myself towards some kind, any kind, of capability.

The bubbling intensified. Something at my wrist—a tugging. Hot, frail fingers. "Don't be dead," he sobbed. "Don't be dead Mommy. Don't be dead."

Come on. He needs you. Wake the fuck up.

I jolted up to a sitting position, letting out a short sharp cry that swallowed Geoff's own scream. Visual intake switched to low panoptics, the world a play of color and shadow. I wasn't fully passed-out or blinded, it was just dark.

Thumping and thundering underneath us. The Trapp core shuddering. All the lights were out, except a few emergency bars drenching us in crimson. My head snapped to the side, and I scanned the bubbling mess that was the remains of Black Hat.

Stupid, getting caught in chemicals even a primary-school baby knows never to mix. It would start exhaling toxic fumes as it ate the hyperalloy in his bones, and his nanos—if any were left undamaged—might be able to patch him up. But not for a long, long while. Bits of reinforced skeleton showed through the soupy mess flesh had turned into. His braincase flashed as the entire wreck shivered, and a tipping rack full of other biochem tubes hovered drunkenly over him.

Those silvery, catslit eyes were still fixed on me, though. There was no mistaking the hate in them, even with eyelids burned away and his thin-lipped face a skeletal ruin.

My scream shuddered to a halt. Geoff tumbled into my arms, and I held him in the dark for a few moments. Sobbing, he shook against me. He kept repeating the same thing.

"I knew you'd come. I knew you'd come. I *knew* it."

I decided not to tell him how close it had been. Ever. Before we got out of here, I needed to pull that rack of tubes down on Black Hat.

It pays to be sure.

"I will always . . ." I had to cough. My nanos moved sluggishly. I needed fuel. "I will *always* come for you."

I shoved at the hatch cover. So did Geoff, muscles straining and eyes bulging. It rose, bit by bit, and fresh air filtered through the crescent of free space.

Something was very wrong, below. The whole complex shuddered; several times we'd almost been thrown off a long ladder leading up a semi-choked pipe. Geoff's arms and legs clenched around me each time, almost cutting off my oxygen, and I hung on grimly. Now, wedged on a narrow platform, I'd found the control pad for this hatch, but there was no emergency power.

It's not going to budge. My flayed feet slipped, a red veil of overstrain closing over my optics as I strained. Geoff whimpered a little.

Amazingly, the hatch suddenly became lighter. I almost fell off the platform, caught Geoff's wrist to keep him on our precarious perch, and pushed it up easily.

That's not quite precise. It was lifted from the other side, too. I peered up, and for a moment I saw pale irises and every bit of adrenaline and cortisol my tired nano-patched glands could scrape together dumped into my bloodstream at once.

Sam leaned over the hatch opening, stretching out and disregarding any kind of defense. His hand cupped empty air. "I'll pull you up."

The familiar steam and sharp green pungency of the Vines poured past us. Below, a large creature growled uneasily.

I bent, Geoff scrambled onto my back again. I reached up, both hands locking around Sam's wrist. His hand turned, caught my left wrist, he braced himself and *pulled.*

My feet hit rough bark-vines. My knees threatened to collapse, I swayed drunkenly, but managed to back up, Geoff clinging to me with his face buried under my hair, his breath a humid spot below my nape.

It wasn't just my exhaustion. The ground itself buckled, heaving like it had decided to pay us back for our tunneling, burrowing, scratching, poking, and slagging.

Sam dropped the hatch back with a hollow clang. I backed up even further. Vines swayed, tree-things whispering as their feet were jostled.

"Genny's gonna blow," Sam informed us. "We should get out of here."

Oh, now it's we? Fat fucking chance. I cleared my throat. "Bastard."

He shrugged. The shocktrooper gear no longer creaked, he'd probably broken it in with some heavy combat, if the splatters of blood and other fluids on him were any indication. He hadn't been topside for very long—there were only a few drops of sap dewing his dirty hair and broad shoulders.

He's bulked out. Facilitators tend to be lean, but he was looking like a liquidator. Where had he found the calories to power that sort of change?

It was a relief to find out I didn't care. Sort of.

He measured me. "Did you kill him?"

I stared at my handler. "You should have told me that was my job."

"It wasn't yours, Abby."

"You. Do *not* ever. Call me that." My throat was a desert. No spare therms here for me to draw on. I'd have to find something to eat, and soon. Even the leaves of the canopy sounded good at this point. My chrono took in the surroundings, decided it didn't need recalibration, and told me it was just a couple hours until dawn.

Thinking of a flood of solar might have made my mouth water. Just a bit.

"All his altered warmbodies collapsed at once. It was pretty amazing."

"And the second-gens?"

He nodded, as if I'd said something profound. "Regrouping. They'll be attended to."

"*They* were your support staff. They heard us in that slag-shack, came in to rescue you from me, and thought you were double-crossing when I kicked the shit out of them. You're playing the corps against the Agency, and both of them against Nikor—if he even exists."

Another shrug, but a very faint smile. Where was the impenetrable handler I'd had? I might have missed him, except he'd turned into this.

Do we ever really know our handlers, though? Sam had been the voice of the Agency to me for years. Who knew what happened when he left a meet with me, or with another one of his agents? How many of them did he *have*?

It wasn't likely that I'd get an answer, but I asked anyway. "Who really owns you?"

The earth shuddered again. It was pretty likely he'd found enough time to sneak around and flip a few switches near the Trapp core. If anything of Black Hat was still moving around inside that sludge, it would be caught in megatons of fused-together rubble. A fossil of technological hatred.

"You wouldn't believe me if I told you." His shoulders dropped. "Go on, Abby. I'll be in touch."

I hesitated. Why?

Geoff trembled against my back. He needed rest. Tired as I was, I could still probably catch a bit of wildlife for him to drain. We were both naked, and had no supplies. No transport. No watermaker.

We'll make do.

"This is it," I told Sam, quietly. I didn't bother to add the threat. *Next time, your head's mine.* "Stay away from us."

"Take care of that kid," he called, just as softly, as I turned and began to jog away with Geoff clinging to my back.

Oh, I intend to.

Warmbody-slow, I stumbled through the Vines. By the time the Trapp core finally blew, we were safely away, and dawn was beginning to tint the falling drops of sap with gold. The Vines shuddered afresh, and Geoff let out a small sound, wiping his mouth as he backed away from the porcine I held by its back legs. I was considering tearing off mouthfuls of raw flesh, and blinked a bit as the force of the reaction groaned in the depths.

"Finish up." I sounded deathly tired even to myself. "Then I'll kiss you goodnight, and you can sleep for a bit."

He nodded, just like the good little boy he was. That haunted look was back in his wide dark eyes.

What would he become?

When he finished drinking, sleepy-eyed and flushed, he nestled in my arms. "I dreamed about them. The silver eyes, and the bad man. They sang until they all fell down."

"I'll just bet they did." I eyed the hulk of the dead porcine, checked the sky. Rapidly lightening. "Find a safe spot, kiddo. We're far enough away that you shouldn't get more than a slight rocking. I'm going to cycle in the sun."

"He'll come back, you know."

No energy to put a subroutine over my autonomics. I didn't bother, although it made my breath catch. "Who?"

"Sam."

"Did you dream that?"

"Mh-hm." A sleepy nod. He pointed at a huge tree, still shivering as the faraway explosion rumbled. There would be a hell of a crater there, but all we'd get here would be aftershocks. "Not for a while, though. When I'm grown."

"Then let's not worry about it now." A fire racing through the Vines was the bigger worry, but not for him underground. At least, I hoped not. I pressed my chapped lips to his filthy forehead. "Okay, kiddo. Go to sleep."

When the earth had sealed itself over my impossible child, I climbed the trunk, too exhausted to even worry about aftershocks *or* flame. The very last of my energy was spent anchoring on a branch high above, one that would catch several hours of misty but strong sunlight. My cheek against rough bark, my naked back a solarcatch panel alive with anticipation as the light strengthened, something occurred to me.

Don't you ever want to burn it down? Black Hat asked again, and I thought it over.

Sure I did.

But I could wait until my kid was grown. By then, I might even have some sort of plan.

With a grateful sigh, I cycled down.

CHAPTER THIRTEEN

CODA

The wheat-haired man crouches in a clearing, his breath a tuneless whistle as he turns a few dials, points the antenna correctly. "Activate relay." A crackling, the scan run through a code or two, time of day and latitude taken into consideration. The machinery picks up a signal, and he stops whistling.

"Code in, please." An anonymous voice, crackling through the small tinny speaker.

"Eight six seven five three oh nine, Jess's Boy, reporting in, foxtrot kilo Juliet, code three-eight."

More crackling. A series of clicks. Then another voice, cold even through the layers of atmosphere and the ancient speaker. "There you are."

Nobody scanned for this transmission range anymore. Sometimes, as the Big Man remarked, the old ways were best.

"Been busy." The man cocks his head, listening intently, to leave no shade or clue unexamined. "CoreTech? The Collective?"

"Both foxed for now." There are broken bodies all around him—rough wooden stakes thrust through the cardiac cavity, heads torn off. "Have already dropped bioscans of their pride and joys, so

at least we get something out of this. Sendoza's Collective process had some regrettable flaws, and the second-gens are no good at fighting crowds." The lies roll easily from his tongue.

"Very good. What about the wolf and her cub?"

Sam doesn't hesitate. "Casualties. Sendoza went nuts, that was always a risk."

A laugh. "Crazy serves our purposes."

"I've burned both CoreTech and the Agency now."

"That also serves our purposes."

So he'd just become expendable. That answered that. "Is there anything that doesn't?"

"Pointless questions."

"Heard and understood."

If you only knew how much I did of both.

"Good. Continue checking in at scheduled intervals. We'll have a use for you soon. Victory out."

The connection is cut, with a small definite snap. Sam sighs. Looks at his blood-covered hands. The Alliance has eyes and ears in every township and City from here to the edge of the continent. Sooner or later someone was going to report Abby and her kid, and Nikor was going to put a couple things together and arrive at a very unpleasant conclusion.

"Not my problem just yet," Sam mutters. It's a relief to be out of the Cities, to let his face relax. The subroutines to keep him a blank-faced nonentity had become second nature. Which was the truth, the blankness or the flickers of feeling?

Did it matter?

Now was the time to get moving. He'd catch up to her, observe from a distance. When—not if—Nikor caught wind of them, the capture orders would come out. And Sam would get another chance to play knight in shining, and maybe earn a little . . . what?

Yes, Nikor was going to be surprised. That didn't happen often, and the Big Man never forgave it, for all his cant about freedom and the future of humanity.

The Agency and corporations, fighting over a dying beast trapped in a waterhole. When the Cities finally broke down, whether under their own weight or as a result of the Alliance's constant efforts at destabilization, Nikor was going to get a few more surprises. The vast mass of agents and corporate slaves weren't going to be grateful for long, and some of them might even want the freeform nanos despite the cost. Lots of warmbodies didn't mind being zombies.

Some of them even preferred it.

Also, Sam had destroyed the bioscans and the details of Sendoza's Collective procedure—but not before memorizing them. Should Abby and that kid get into trouble, he could trade dribs and drabs of it to get them out.

"Who owns me now, AbbyJess?" He smiled, and straightened. Time to get the blood off his hands. "Who do you think?"

He made sure the bloated bodies would catch sunlight. The blast zone, here where the original Libera—once, long ago, an Alliance township, then one of Nikor's experiments gone hideously wrong, now a steaming crater—once stood, was the perfect place to leave these little presents. As long as nobody took the stakes out, the second-gens would rot quietly.

Of course, if they didn't, he had a plan for that too. So many to keep track of, crowding his active brain. A Facilitator couldn't be caught unprepared.

With that done, he destroyed the relay. No more call-ins. His next one wasn't due for a couple months, anyway.

"Who owns me now." He kicked the relay's useless hulk one more time for good measure. "I do, sweets. You're a bad influence."

Five minutes later, the clearing was empty.

Two hours after that, one of the scattered, headless bodies twitched once. Twice.

The Vines sighed. Aftershocks rippled through its roots. The sun rose higher.

And the headless body twitched again . . .

ABOUT THE AUTHOR

Lilith Saintcrow was born in New Mexico. She fell in love with writing in the second grade and has continued obsessively ever since. Saintcrow has penned more than twenty-five novels and is perhaps best known for her Dante Valentine and Jill Kismet series, as well as her current Hostage to Empire series, written as S. C. Emmett. Read more about the author on www.lilithsaintcrow.com.

LILITH SAINTCROW

FROM OPEN ROAD MEDIA

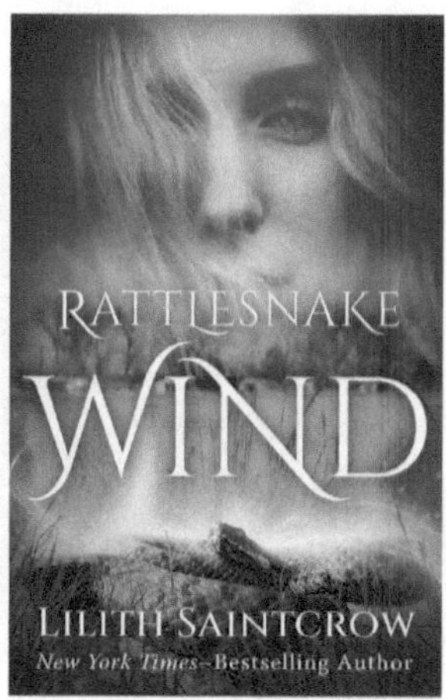

OPEN ROAD
INTEGRATED MEDIA

www.ingramcontent.com/pod-product-compliance
Lightning Source LLC
LaVergne TN
LVHW090602110826
845146LV00001B/234

9798337208381